A Time of Disillusion

Book 5 in the Bovey Tracey Saga

**The Continuing Story of a
West Country Town
Following the Civil War**

Jim Marshall

Front cover image:
Edward Hyde, First Earl of Clarendon.
Attributed to Master Style

ISBN:978-1-918038-27-9

This book is in very fond memory of

HENRY WILLIAMSON

A writer of immense power and feeling.
Despite his political leanings,
I am indebted to him.

CONTENTS

CAST OF MAIN CHARACTERS

<u>Town of Bovey Tracey</u>

Church	Rev. James Forbes
Tavern	Dick and Sal Allen
Blacksmith	Simon Smith, wife Imelda, son Jack, daughter Rachael
Bookseller	Gaston Bessant, wife Glory, daughter Isobel.
Apothecary	James Ramsey, wife Avril, apprentice Rosie Ramsey
Growers	Gil Ramsey, wife Ella, son Jamie
School	Lou Crowley – caretaker. Felix – adopted son

<u>Parke Estate</u>

Steward	Luke Barton, wife Grace
Bailiff	Harry Cove, wife Mary (also schoolteacher), twins Will and Peterkin, daughter Lauren
Deputy	Hob Slater, wife May, daughters Kitty and Poppy
Staff	Sam Garvey, Robert Hook, Bernie Wheatcroft (shepherd)

<u>Brimley Estate</u>

Owner	Paul Larkin ex-parliamentary colonel
Custodians	Peter and Laura Cove
Steward	Luke Farmer, wife Meg, son Hal
Staff	Kit Warden (gardener)
Resident	Matthew Kent (large cottage)

<u>Newton Abbot</u>

Ship owner	Adam Clements, wife Nell, daughter Kate. Servant Lottie

<u>Trusham</u>

Michael Brown and Hugh Ratcliffe (hurdle makers)

<u>Others</u>

Colonel Fisher – ex parliamentary officer

King Charles II

Queen Catherine (of Braganza)

Lord Clarendon

Sir Thomas Cartwright – sheriff of Devon

INTRODUCTION

The year is 1666, it is early October. Charles Stuart had been Charles II of Scotland ever since his father's execution in 1649. Despite help from the Scots, he had been finally defeated by Cromwell at Worcester on 3rd September 1651.

He spent much of the intervening years in the Netherlands, fathering at least four illegitimate children. Then on that same 3rd September, but in the year 1658, Cromwell had died, leaving his son Richard (Tumbledown Dick) in charge. That lasted only a short time until General Lambert had taken over – first with a parliament and then with his army.

General George Monck had ousted Lambert – who had not paid his army and who deserted him. The old 'Rump' Parliament had been reinstated in 1660 and had invited Charles to return as king – but with some restrictions. Charles, with his principal advisor Edward Hyde, had issued the Declaration of Breda, in which he agreed to tolerance of religious observation, a general amnesty for all those who recognised his right to be king, a proper settlement of land disputes, and full arrears of pay for the army.

Nothing had been said about the general amnesty being applied to those who had signed his father's death warrant – and had thereby *not* recognised Charles I as rightful king.

Many of the regicides had been arrested and executed. Cromwell's body had been exhumed, his head cut off and displayed as would have happened to any traitor. Many people were disgusted at that action.

Charles had taken as his queen a young princess from Portugal – Catherine of Braganza. That did not preclude the fathering of more bastards!

And then, in 1665 had come the huge Plague of London. At least 70,000 had perished; many put the number closer to 100,000.

Finally, on 2nd September 1666, a massive fire had started in Pudding Lane. When it was final extinguished (or had burned itself out) eighty percent of the city had been utterly destroyed.

And so, back to Bovey Tracey a month after the fire.

CHAPTER I

A rather tired and somewhat bedraggled horse clumped its way up the main street of the town of Bovey Tracey. In the saddle sat an equally tired and bedraggled young man, his head nodding now and again as he tried to fend off a tendency to drop off to sleep. It had been a rather long and tiring ride.

Arrived at long last at the tavern, he slid to the ground and handed his mount to the tavern's ostler, who regarded the poor animal with some dismay.

"You'm done the poor bugger in!" he snorted at the young rider, who looked in as sorry a state as the horse.

"Aye, and sorry I am for the pair of us. I'll stay with my parents until the morrow. But first, I am in dire need of a few gallons of ale." So saying, he walked around to the front of the tavern and into the large taproom.

"Dear God above – look what the cat has dragged in – and looking in as sorry a state as the mouse in its jaws!" Dick Allen, now a greying and grizzled fifty-five years old, tavern owner, came over and gave the young man a pat on his shoulder. Looking over his shoulder, he bellowed for his wife. Sal Allen, two years younger than her husband, came hurrying from the kitchens.

"Dear Lord bless us – tis Jamie, and in a state not fit to be seen. Come away in and sit."

Sal bustled away and ordered a large mug of ale for the young man – who slumped onto a bench and greedily gulped down the mugful. He grinned up at Dick.

"I needed that," he said, folded his arms on the table and went to sleep.

Dick, beckoning his small tavern boy, told the lad to hurry down to the smallholding and summon either Gil or Ella, and to say that their son was needing a bath, a change of clothes, a massive meal, and a bed – and probably in that order. He gave an expansive grin to his other patrons – most of whom had known Jamie since his birth – and left the young man to his slumbers.

It was half an hour later when the door opened again to reveal the tavern boy and a slim young woman dressed in a work gown with a white apron on top. She simply went over to Jamie, grabbed a handful of his hair and tugged it.

"Wake up. You look horrible!" she said by way of greeting.

"And you, dear sister, look as ugly as ever," Jamie retorted, one eye still closed.

That remark in no way was warranted, just the banter between brother and sister. Rosie, a full-grown nineteen and two years her brother's senior, was not ugly. She was not beautiful either – not in the accepted version of beautiful. She had a pert nose inherited from her mother, a few freckles, and a mass of wavy hair that fell well below the line of her shoulders. She was serious, dedicated to her work, and the object of many a young man's glances. Jamie was taller, swarthy, and strong of body, like many wiry young men who lived in the countryside.

"I suppose I have to get you back to mama and papa," Rosie pouted. "Though, heaven alone knows what they will make of the condition you are in."

"I have stories to tell that will keep everyone entranced for many an hour," Jamie grinned, getting to his feet. With a wave of thanks to Dick, he followed Rosie out of the door to start on the walk down the street to the smallholding where his parents lived – and where he had lived until two years previously.

"You shall have to summon all the family to hear my tale," he said as they neared the large cottage, the large vegetable garden and chicken run stretching far down onto the Heath behind it. "All need to hear what we have discovered."

Almost at the top of the main street, on the right, was the bakery. For many years it had been the domain of John and Evelyn Ramsey. Their son Gil was Rosie's and Jamie's father. Now in their mid-fifties and retired, John and Evelyn lived in a small cottage about a mile south of the town on the road past the Heath that led to Newton Abbot. The bakery had been sold some two years previously to Gerald Shooter, who now ran it with the help of two young apprentices and a lad of twelve. Somehow or other, the high standard of bread and cakes had been maintained, but not without the sudden outbursts of very colourful language that had most people grinning – even Reverend James Forbes, who lived not that far away on the other side of the road next to the church. That day was to be no exception.

"Damnation, hell and buggery!" came a shout from the rear of the baker shop, where the ovens and mixing, proving, and shaping took place.

"What is amiss, master?" one of the young apprentices looked into the rear room from where he had been stacking new loaves in the shop.

"What is amiss, you ask? This bloody bread shovel be amiss, that's what!" The offending long-handled tool was hurled to the far wall where the handle snapped off.

"Now look!" bellowed Shooter. "Tis now less than useless!"

"Why do we not ask Simon to fashion us a new blade out of iron, then get a stout wooden handle affixed?" the young fellow repeated what he had recommended many days past.

"Twill cost coin, that's why not!"

"But without it, how may you take bread from the ovens?"

"Shit and buggery! Take the blade and carve off that piece that sticks up. I shall somehow nail the handle back when you are done."

"Won't work," the apprentice whispered to his young colleagues.

The next morning, he was proved right. The volume and scope of the curses startled even Simon the blacksmith – and he was used to his father's language!

About sixteen miles to the west – and a trifle north - of Bovey Tracey, Paul Larkin sat quite comfortably inside the stone remains of what had been a home for someone who had lived (and presumably worked) on the moor. It was no casual and indiscriminate arrangement of granite blocks; they had been deliberately chosen and piled so as to make the round walls of a hut. Sheep droppings littered the entrance, but few had encroached inside. The roof, whatever had been its construction, had long since collapsed. Larkin sat inside and marvelled at the ingenuity of the man who had originally fashioned the hut. He believed it to be some two thousand years old.

About a quarter of a mile to the north stood a craggy, granite tor. Another was further away to the east. Larkin sat and munched his way through a heel of bread and some cheese. On his lap was a sheaf of papers. His assistant, Jamie, had meticulously written down the finds of the previous three days – a stone circle, various stone and iron tools, even the remains of a bronze brooch. Larkin's purpose was to write a definitive account of the moor, along with as accurate map as he could manage. In the saddle bag was his compass. His horse, tethered very loosely on a long rein scrabbled to find grass that was edible.

Larkin, until six years previously, had been a colonel in the New Model Army. Various tasks had taken him to South Devon – murder and plots against the state – where he had come to realise that this was where he wanted to spend the rest of his life. His home was in Brimley, a small hamlet just to the west of Bovey Tracey. He had purchased Brimley Manor following the death of its previous owner, the hugely respected and much missed Lady Violette Charlton.

Two buzzards were circling above the nearest tor, looking ready to swoop down on some unsuspecting small animal. A small herd of wild ponies grazed contentedly down towards one of the myriad streams and rivers that crossed the moor. In the far distance, he could see spirals of smoke coming from the fires around Hay Tor where granite was being quarried. This was a quite recent innovation, one that Larkin was determined to study and write about.

He sat back and uttered a sigh of contentment, quite happy to await Jamie's return the next day with further provisions. He gave not one thought to his estate in Brimley. He knew that it was in the safe and capable hands of Peter and Laura Cove, and Luke and Meg Farmer. Peter and Laura were his live-in custodians, whilst Luke and Meg were steward and housekeeper/cook. Larkin was quietly content with life.

That evening, Rosie had gathered as many of the family as possible to hear Jamie's news. Their parents, Gil and Ella Ramsey, Gil's sister Mary, her husband Harry the Bailiff, and their twins, Will and Peterkin. These lads, now fourteen, were insanely jealous of their cousin Jamie for his chance of an adventure whilst they were kept busy at the Parke Estate. The final members of the gathering were Simon Smith, Ella's brother and the town blacksmith, Imelda, Simon's wife, and Jack their son and assistant blacksmith, plus Rachael their daughter who spent her time assisting Mary at the school.

"So, Jamie," Mary opened proceedings as befitted the town's schoolmistress. "What tales have you to relate?"

"Since I was last here in the middle of September, we have concentrated mainly on the area north of Ashburton. It is probably the hardest to map so far as it is dotted with small tors, stands of trees, little river valleys, and even the remains of a very old castle. It took us three whole weeks to cover an area no larger than a quarter of a square mile!"

"Wow!" young Will was immediately interested. "That old castle – what? Walls, moat, towers and everything?"

"Nay – none of those," Jamie laughed. "Completely overgrown now. But it showed signs of the traditional motte and bailey, though on a very small scale. The keep was probably wooden and has completely rotted away. But we found a few items buried deep in the leaf litter – a rusty spear head, a couple of eating bowls, and a brooch. The Colonel believes they were from well before the Conqueror."

"1066!" Peterkin was the first to blurt out his knowledge. "That is precisely six hundred years past. But this place was before that?"

"Aye – or so the Colonel believes. He said it could be well before Saxon times – perhaps as far back as Celtic."

"That would mean it could be before our Christian faith was brought here," Rachael was immediately interested. "How wonderful would it be if we could see them, hear them speak, watch them at work. Not that we would be able to understand them, of course. Their language would have been akin to Welsh or Cornish."

Mary gave her assistant a look of pride. Rachael was slowly becoming a very learned young woman. Now a quiet, fifteen-year-old, she had a thirst for knowledge, plus a compendious memory for even the smallest fact. She also shunned the advances of every red-blooded young man. As she had confided to Mary once, she would countenance only a young man her equal in thirst for knowledge, impeccable manners, and very good prospects. Mary wondered where she might find such a person!

Jamie went on to relate other finds – flint tools, very rusty old swords, cooking pots, and various remains of stone dwellings. "The Colonel says that we shall come down from the moor in a few weeks from now as the folk who live up there foretell yet another bad winter!"

"Thank the Good Lord you did not stay up there last winter," Rosie replied. "It was a very bad one and we were rushed off our feet for many weeks tending the sick!"

Rosie, now nineteen and still unmarried, had been assistant to James and Avril Ramsey, the town apothecaries. Well able to attend patients herself, she had diagnosed, prescribed, and tended many of the sick herself and knew that another bad winter would see off those who had barely managed to survive the last one.

"I shall ride back up on the morrow," Jamie reported. "I shall take just enough provisions to last us four weeks."

Peterkin, thoughtful where his twin was impetuous, posed the last question. "What shelter do you have up there? Is it still what you called it last time, a bivvy-whack?"

"It is called a bivouac!" Rachael snorted. "It is a French word that came from an original German word, 'biwacht'. It means a place where a guard shelters."

"Ye Gods!" Simon whispered to his sister Ella. "I have sired a bloody genius!"

The final meeting of that evening was held in the parlour of the rectory. The church of Saints Peter, Paul, and Thomas was unique in that it was dedicated to three people. Peter and Paul were quite common names for a church. Thomas had been added many years before by Baron deTracey. He not only gave his name to the town but added the third dedication as he had been one of the assassins of Thomas Becket in Canterbury!

The Reverend James Forbes, now well into his sixties, presided. Forbes had been chaplain to the then Prince Charles – now King Charles II – during the civil war. His two guests were Matthew Kent, a retired parliamentary agent, and Colonel Fisher – once a senior officer under Fairfax and Cromwell.

The three, along with Paul Larkin, had formed themselves into a debating group that they had styled The Sane and Sensible.

"Well, first item to be debated is the excellence of this wine," Forbes raised his glass to the flames from the fire to appreciate the deep ruby glinting within.

Fisher, who had donated three bottles for the meeting, grunted his appreciation. "Bought it from a chappie who has opened a shop in Chudleigh. He swears it originates from the Burgundians."

"Wherever it comes from, it is indeed excellent," Kent took another sip, rolling it around his tongue. "Aha – a hint of blackberry!"

"Nay! Blackcurrant!" Forbes argued. "Nevertheless, we all agree upon its superb quality. Now – Fisher – what of London and the court?"

Fisher, who was visited regularly by messengers from the capital, cleared his throat.

"Plans are being drawn up for the complete re-building of London – especially St. Paul's and the other churches that were incinerated. A chap called Wren seems to have some grandiose plan that he is hawking around various offices. Won't be the same old London, though!"

"Then, may the saints be praised for that," Kent laughed. "The old city was in a terrible state. It has taken the deaths of many thousand souls to bring about the end of squalor, filth, and evil smells."

"What of the court? Any news?" Forbes probed.

"Aye and none that I would call good news," Fisher grunted. "Charles has made his first bastard son Duke of Monmouth! His other three sired before his restoration – well, one died in infancy and the other two are flourishing. His latest mistress, Barbara Villers, has already presented him with Anne, Charles, Henry,

Charlotte, and George. That makes nine illegitimate children he has sired so far. His father would be by now turning in his grave! As for our dear king's wife, nothing so far. Poor Catherine seems unable to produce a child."

"But if she did, we would have a problem on our hands!" Kent argued. "Catherine from Braganza in Portugal is a devout Catholic. Would not she insist on their child also be one of that religion?"

"Indeed – that would put Charles in the proverbial cleft stick," Forbes nodded. "He is already beholden to the Scottish Covenanters, to the English Church which he swore to maintain at his coronation. Catherine, being a Catholic, may not be crowned queen, although she is the queen consort by right of marriage."

Fisher prefaced his next remark with one of his prodigious grunts. "Religion would seem to be far from the forefront of his mind! The court is a riot of revels, masques, secret rendezvous, lasciviousness, and intrigue. There could be no greater difference from the court of his straightlaced father!"

"Or from the years of rule by Parliament!" Kent added.

"We swing from chaos through to chaos!" Forbes agreed. "First, we have a king who claimed divine rule; then we have a parliament violently opposed to the king, leading to years of war. Then we have the rule of parliament with its puritanical laws and regulations. Now we swing in the opposite direction where merrymaking and permissiveness seem to be the order of the day. When, I wonder, will England again come to its senses under calm and thoughtful leadership?"

"Not under Merry Charles, that's for certain!" Fisher concluded that debate.

CHAPTER II

Adam Clements finished his breakfast porridge, drained his mug of weak ale, wiped his lips, and rose from the table in the large parlour. That room, plus two bedchambers and a storeroom, were situated above the large office premises and a workroom that formed the ground floor of the large house.

"Is your mama down in her workroom already?" he asked the golden-haired little girl who was sitting on a high stool as she also finished her smaller bowl.

"Aye, papa. Mama went down before you were awake."

Adam grinned to himself. He might have known that his wife would be busy from first light until it became too dark to see her work. Not that Nell disregarded their daughter – she often had little Kate down with her showing her all the different herbs and roots that she worked on to keep the apothecaries and physicians supplied with the necessary. A tousled head poked around the door.

"May I clear up, master?" it asked.

"Aye – we are all finished," Adam replied, waving into the room a small figure dressed in a large child's dress and pinafore. Lottie was a foundling – just eleven years of age whom Nell had discovered dressed in rags and begging outside the small hall where the merchants and senior traders met every month. Nell being Nell had brought the girl into their home, dressed her in clothes from a good draper, and had slowly elicited her story.

It appeared that Lottie had been born not that far away in a hamlet called Netherton. Her father, a poor fisherman, and her mother, had died six years previously from what was still called the winter fever. Five-year-old Lottie had been thrown on her own resources. For a couple of years, she had been fed by the tiny parish. Then, she had walked the few miles all on her own to the town of Newton Abbot, where she had existed by begging ever since.

Lottie had been with the Clements family for just on a year. In that time, she had proved herself invaluable, doing the washing, cooking, and acting as nursemaid to little Kate – who she adored. In return for bed and board, Lottie worked tirelessly for Nell and Adam, who she also adored.

Adam planted a kiss on top of Kate's mass of curls, then went downstairs to see his wife.

"I shall be gone for most of the day," he announced. "There is a large consignment coming down for loading this morning – and I want to see it safely stowed away before the ship sails with the evening tide."

Nell looked up from her large worktable, pausing in her work of chopping arrowroot into tiny slivers. Not only did she supply medicines and specifics, she was consulted by all and sundry as her medical knowledge was profound. Also, she never prescribed bleeding a patient. Her mentors, James and Avril Ramsey in Bovey Tracey, had always said that blood was in the body for a purpose, and it was better kept within!

"Take care on the roads. They will be slippery after so much rain," she came around to bestow a kiss on her husband's cheek.

"Aye – careful and with sorrow to be away from you for yet another full day," he smiled down at his wife. He shouldered his large leather bag and walked down three more buildings to where his faithful horse was stabled. Lucky, saddled and fed, was waiting for him. Lucky was the name he had given to the horse some years before when it had escaped unhurt from a stable fire that had taken its dam and three other horses.

The road towards Teignmouth was indeed slippery. Holes that were filled with muddy water had to be avoided as nobody could tell how deep they were. One misstep could lame a horse. The journey to the small jetty at the eastern bank of the river Teign was crowded. Five ships were moored there. Adam owned three ships. One was there at the jetty; another was returning from London; the third was half-way to Hull on the Yorkshire coast. He hailed the master of his ship and together they repaired to a nearby tavern to talk through the load and the voyage – also to London, where frantic building was consuming every block of granite that could be delivered.

The granite made a perilous journey down from Hay Tor, then was transferred to small barges near Bovey Tracey, to the jetty at Teignmouth. Adam and his father – also a ship owner operating from nearer to Plymouth – had managed to grab a slice of this burgeoning business. It had proved extremely profitable.

Jacob Winter, master of the ship Fair Nell, was squat, tanned and had the rolling gait that spoke of many years at sea. He gulped down the first half of his mug of ale. Details of the cargo and voyage settled, he then started upon his favourite occupation – disseminating information that he had acquired from his many nautical sources. Some of these proved to be remarkably accurate!

"A cog from Brizz'l were in two days past," he started.

Adam rightly construed this to be the local Devon pronunciation of Bristol.

"Never guess what its master told us!" Winter gave his boss a grin.

Adam, well used to this goading, looked at his ship master with interest.

"That new trade we all hear about from Brizz'l and Liverpool!"

"Aye – what of it?"

"'Tis said that they sail all the way to the African coast taking trinkets and poorly made firearms, use these to trade for black slaves, pack the buggers tight into the holds, then cross the seas to the sugar islands, sell the slaves to the masters, load with sugar and spices, then sail back to their home ports."

Adam was silent for a while, digesting this latest item of gossip. Could it have any grain of truth in it? Many questions occurred to him.

"First, many would die on such a voyage," he made his first objection. "Such losses would make the trade worthless!"

"Nay – I hear tell that only one in ten fails to arrive. Anyhow, they be only black heathens!"

Adam was not sure that this argument was sound.

"Black and heathen they might be. But they are still of God's creation!" he argued.

"No better than the beasts of the field – or so that master told me! And we have enslaved cattle to our needs for centuries!"

"You only just heard of this trade?" came a deep voice from a nearby table. "I heard of it many moons past!"

The voice belonged to a huge man dressed like Winter as a ship's master. Adam recognised him as master of a large cog that sailed regularly between Teignmouth and the French ports. Adam also knew that there was fierce rivalry between ship's masters for telling of the latest intelligence – be it fact or mere rumour.

"Tis said they Portuguese have been at it for many a year!" the man continued. "Not surprising some of our own traders want a slice of the profits!"

"But is it a Christian thing to do – trade in people?" Adam asked.

"Why not?" the giant argued. "We trade in wool, wines, granite, anything that the Good Lord put upon this earth. How be black heathens any different?"

Adam said nothing, merely digested the information – if that was in fact what it really was. The rest of his day was spent supervising the loading and safe stowage of many tons of granite, then riding back to his home – still deep in thought.

That evening when Kate had been told her story and put to bed – Lottie in close attendance in the smaller bedchamber – Adam related to Nell what he had heard. He was unsurprised by her immediate reaction.

"Tis sinful!" Nell exclaimed. "Just imagine our feelings were some people to invade our home, steal away our little Kate, then transport her hundreds of miles distant to be a slave to some despicable master!"

"But they would have no use for children!" Adam argued. "Surely, they would want only strong, grown men for the work that awaited them!"

"Then, imagine this. Kate and I left alone when *you* were taken from us. Tis no different! Tis sinful *whoever* is taken!"

"Aye, you have it right – as usual!" Adam nodded. It was what his innermost thoughts had told him anyway.

In bed that night, he turned matters over again and again. What, he wondered, would the people of England make of it, should they ever be informed? After all, their uncrowned queen was Portuguese!

Did his father know of this trade? It would be a safe bet that he did as there was little in the shipping business that his father did *not* know. If so, why had he never mentioned it? Was it because he feared that his son would disagree? Or, heaven forbid, that he feared that his son would want to join in! It was with these jumbled thoughts that Adam finally fell asleep.

CHAPTER III

Kitty Slater was twelve, her sister Poppy a mere ten. They were two of the oldest children attending the town's school. They lived with their parents, Hob and May Slater, at Parke estate where Hob was deputy estate and town bailiff. The two girls sat together at the very back of the classroom as Mary Cove believed that they were also two of the most trustworthy.

The school, half-way up the main street, was named The Lady Violette Charlton School – after the much loved and hugely respected old lady who had bought and brought back to life the nearby estate at Brimley. She had died some years before leaving, as part of her bequests the money to buy the freehold of the school outright, plus a further fund to defray running costs for many years into the future. She had also left another fund to supply bursaries for children whose parents could not afford the small school fees.

Mary Cove, now thirty-four years of age, had been schoolteacher ever since the school had started. Married to Harry Cove, the bailiff, she was the mother of Will and Peterkin, twins of fourteen, and Lauren, now nine - and another of her pupils. Even her own children referred to her as 'Miss Mary' when at school.

There were another thirteen children at the school, ranging in age from eight to May's eldest at twelve. Mary had decided upon a lesson in the form of a debate for that morning.

"Today, we shall discuss pixies," she announced, causing one hand immediately to be raised in the back row.

"But we have all been told that they do not exist!" Kitty blurted out.

"And that is precisely why we will discuss them," Mary gave Kitty a broad smile. "Not to argue that they *do* exist, but to think about why some people believe that they do. So, can anyone think of other examples?"

"Hobgoblins!" came the immediate answer from one of the young boys from the Heath. "My grandmother is always blaming them for hiding things that she has misplaced!"

"Ghosts and Spectres!" came from Lauren. "Bernie the shepherd swears he sees them when he is tending the sheep on a very dark night."

"I think we have enough to go on with," Mary held up a hand to stem what could well become an avalanche of weird beings. "Now, has anyone any idea why some folk believe in them?"

That was met with a baffled silence. Sixteen faces were screwed up in frowns that Mary found quite illuminating. She was always posing questions for them to ponder, forcing them to think problems through. Eventually, Poppy raised her hand.

"Did people believe in them before our Christian faith was brought here?" she faltered, wondering whether she had broached a forbidden subject.

"Oh, I'm sure they did," Mary nodded. "But does that explain why some people *still* believe in them?"

"Perhaps those people have not properly understood that God created the world and everything in it – and there is no mention of pixies, hobgoblins, or spectres in the Bible! Therefore, God did *not* create them – so they cannot exist!" came from a normally quiet boy, son of a farmer from the Heath.

"That is a very plausible explanation. Can anyone else think of another reason?"

More silence.

"I think that God is not a very kind person," one lad spoke up. "Mistress Hopkins told me that God sends plague to the cities because we are wicked, and that he will smite me down if I play outside her house! Why would God do that?"

"Oh, believe me – He would do no such thing!" Mary laughed. "You were doing what children do everywhere in the world. They play and find things to do that are fun. There is nothing at all wicked in that. Disregard anything that Mistress Hopkins says. She and her brother are just miserable old lummocks!"

That caused a lot of laughter. The Hopkins were strict Puritans who saw nothing but evil everywhere they looked – and they *did* look everywhere.

"So, pixies do not really exist," Poppy stated firmly, bringing the discussion back to where it had started.

"Miss Mary – what happens to us when we die?"

Mary looked, she hoped, supremely confident as she prepared to answer that question. It had nothing whatsoever to do with the pixies and other, miscellaneous beings. But she knew that she could neither dodge the question nor give some flippant answer. One small hand in the front row was raised.

"Please, Miss Mary, Reverend Forbes told us that our souls go to Jesus when we die. But he didn't tell us what our souls really are!"

Mary knew full well that she was treading on very dangerous ground. But she wasn't regarded as the town's reference point for nothing.

"Rab – go out to the small field opposite and find a flower and bring it back in here. It matters not which flower – there will be a few left."

Wondering what on earth he was supposed to make of that, young Rab scampered off to do as bid. Mary folded her arms and waited patiently for the lad to return. The door burst open and young Rab handed Mary a somewhat mangled light purple anemone that he had found by a hedgerow. Undaunted, Mary thanked Rab and held it up.

"Now, I want you to look at this flower and tell me what you see – all the different bits of it."

The answers ranged from petals, stalk, little leaves, to funny 'little middle bits'.

"Aye, those are the parts of the flower we can all see," Mary nodded. "But what else do we see when we look at it as a whole?"

Deafening silence until Poppy raised her hand at the back.

"Please, Miss Mary – is it the beauty of it?"

Mary placed the flower on her desk and gave Poppy a big grin.

"Aye – *that* is what we see. Can we touch it, this beauty? Can we explain it? It is the same with us. We are a mixture of skin, bones, muscles, blood, wriggly bits inside, eyes, nose, mouth, teeth – in some cases, even a brain! We can see all of these things. We can touch them. They exist for us all to see. But what about what we cannot see? Our thoughts, our likes and dislikes? We cannot see them, can we. But they exist. Can you actually *see* or touch the taste of a piece of mouldy cheese? Of course, we cannot. But it certainly exists! Now, most of us have known people we have loved and have died – especially those taken by the winter fevers. Now that they are gone from us, we cannot see them. But close your eyes tight shut and *imagine* that person. Then we can see him or her as clear as daylight. But we still cannot touch them. They exist in our memories. What we see in our brains is the external features that we remember. What we also see is the memory of who that person was. And that is as close as any of us are ever likely to get to the soul of that person. It is the *essence* of what they were. Nobody can see, touch, smell or hear it. But it exists. The sum of that person's life is what goes up to Jesus in heaven. We happen to call it a soul. I prefer to call it the essence of that person. No matter what we call it, it is there – and you have all now experienced what I'm talking about by thinking of that person who is no longer alive for us to see."

"Wow," Poppy exclaimed. "But what if the person we are remembering was a bad person?"

"It matters not one whit!" Mary replied with a smile. "The essence is still there, be it good or bad. Now, how many of you remember Nell who was with my Uncle James in the apothecary shop?"

A few hands went up.

"Nell's mama died as she gave birth to her. Her papa died when she was but four years old. But every week, without fail, she would go to her papa's grave and talk to him. He was not there to hear her, nor could she see him. But she spoke to that essence that she remembered so well. She would pray for him and her mama. That essence of her papa is still there!"

"I pray to God every night," Rab broke in. "But so do thousands of others. God must have very big ears to hear all of us!"

Mary pretended not to hear that. Omnipotence was not a subject that she was going to discuss with little children!

"Now – enough for one morning. Off you go to your dinners. This afternoon, each of you is going to write a little story telling about someone who has died and that you remember – and *why* you remember them."

Poppy went home for her dinner with her sister, still somewhat perplexed.

"Still does not explain about pixies!" she muttered.

CHAPTER IV

October, which had been changeable, gave way to a November that started off with a cold wind and brilliant, clear skies. It was this that encouraged Larkin to stay another week up on the moor.

He and Jamie had plotted as much as they could in the area north of Ashburton. They had jointly decided to concentrate next upon a very small area slightly further west where the tiny hamlet of Babeny was situated. The area was criss-crossed by lots of tiny streams that at first proved very difficult to map.

"Why did Almighty God in all His wisdom not create these bloody things in straight lines?" Jamie fumed as the one they were following did yet another ninety degree turn to avoid a small granite outcrop. Using a prominent tor as reference, he took a bearing with the compass and paced out the next 'leg' of the little stream.

"Tis not as if the wretched thing will even follow the same course in ten years from now," Larkin grinned at Jamie's obvious frustration. It would be another year, he thought, and Jamie would be one of the finest plotters in the country.

"Please tell me that you are not planning another expedition in ten years to see where the cursed thing then is!" Jamie pleaded.

"It may not even be in existence," Larkin laughed aloud. "Further back, it may have joined with another and ceased to exist hereabouts. What we are doing is making a map for others to refer to – to see what *used* to be. Tis invaluable information."

At the next turn of the little stream, Jamie again took a bearing so that his tracing of the course would be as accurate as possible. He had taken no more than ten paces along that new leg when his eye was caught by a larger than usual 'pixie' hole.

He finished pacing out towards the next bend, then returned to peer into the deep hole. And he stopped dead in his tracks.

"Colonel – bones in here – and they look like as if they are part of a human skeleton," he called out to Larkin who was busy examining a clump of gorse where the remnants of sheep's wool were caught. He looked up at the shout.

"Are you sure they are human bones?" he asked.

"Got a skull, two shoulders, loads of ribs and two arms that I can see," Jamie replied.

Larkin joined him at the lip of the hole and peered down into its depths.

"Aye, one human skeleton. Wonder how long it has been in there? Are you prepared to go down and see what else may be nestling in the hole?"

"Aye, I'm not afraid of bones," Jamie grinned. Larkin looped a rope about Jamie's waist so that he could help to haul him back up again. Jamie went over to the side away from the bones and clambered down into the hole. First, he examined the skull.

"Big crack in the left side," he called up. "Might have been clouted before he fell in – or he may have fallen on a rock himself." He rummaged through the debris at the bottom of the hole. "Feet still in leather boots," he called again.

"You say 'he'," Larkin shouted down. "Could it not be 'she'?"

"Nay – those boots look mighty like a soldier's boots. Hello – what is this?"

His rummaging had unearthed a leather covered bottle, the leather thick with mould. He peered at the side of the flat container. "Tis a name burned into it."

Larkin hauled Jamie up and they both examined the find. The letters were hard to make out, but both agreed that they spelled a name.

"Herrick," Larkin grunted. "I wonder who he was."

Mary walked home after school with her daughter. The afternoon had gone surprisingly well, all the children having submitted a short story about someone that they remembered - and why they remembered them. Mary had been very gratified to see the continuing standard of written English, spelling and (in some cases) correct punctuation.

"Did you like my story?" Lauren asked as she skipped along beside her mother.

"Yes, it was very well written. I did not know that you were acquainted with Samuel Wooley."

"He was the one who chased the twins away from his cows. Twas about a year ago and he was very angry."

"But you wrote how nice he was!"

"Aye – to me, he was nice. He gave me two pennies not to tell you and papa about him chasing the twins."

Mary decided that a short lecture was in order, but not before she again upbraided her daughter on her spoken English.

"Lauren, sweetie – you should say 'yes' and 'no' – not 'aye' and 'nay'. You should also say 'it was' and not 'twas'."

"But mama – they mean the same thing!"

"Yes, I know they do. But the words you use are not correct."

Lauren said nothing aloud. Silently, she mouthed 'don't care', but made sure her mother neither heard nor saw her lips move.

"Now," Mary knew she had to strike whilst the iron was hot. "You should never accept pennies from anyone ever again. Certainly not from someone like Master Wooley."

"Why not, mama? Shall I never be allowed to take pennies from you and dada?"

"I did not mean from your family. I meant from anyone who you do not know properly. They might want you to do things in return."

"What? Like milk his cows?"

Mary decided to leave well alone for the time being. She would have to keep a closer eye on her young, trusting daughter – and that made her rather sad.

Colonel Fisher arrived at the Bovey Rectory that evening in a state of some confusion. What he had heard recently had given him much food for thought. He needed to use his sounding-board – Reverend James Forbes. In the past, they had always made some sort of sense out of their discussions.

"What brings you here in such a lather?" Forbes greeted his old friend. "Come away in and have a glass of wine – and then tell me what it is all about."

Fisher sank into his usual chair and took a tentative sip of the wine – a cool and refreshing white Bordeaux. He gave a grunt of satisfaction before starting on his news.

"It is common knowledge that our king has already sired nine illegitimate children – using first Lucy Walter, Catherine Pegge, Elizabeth Killigrew, and the wretched Villiers woman – styled the Duchess of Cleveland. Well – according to intelligence that I personal regard as near to gospel, the king is tiring of Villiers and is seen in the company of a damned actress. My informant tells me that Master Pepys – who is in the know about most things – refers to her as 'pretty, witty, Nell'. Her proper name is Eleanor Gwynne – although she goes by the name Nell. It is, I suppose, barely conceivable that the king consort with a duchess – but an actress? Surely, this cannot be tolerated?"

Forbes listened with resignation as his old friend listed Charles' conquests. He hesitated to pronounce any judgement on a king he had known from a very young man. Instead, he veered at a tangent.

"Before Parliament closed the theatres, all female roles were taken by juvenile actors – or actors who were of a particular bent. Now that the places are open again, it would appear that females are being encouraged by some circles to display their own talents upon the boards."

"James – you are transparent! Pray comment upon the king and an actress."

"I hesitate to do so," Forbes shrugged. "After all, Lucy Walter who birthed his first child, was hardly of noble stock!"

"No matter how good she may be upon the stage – and I hear that she is very good indeed – she cannot be considered fit company for a crowned king. What his wife may think of all this is beyond my comprehension!"

"From what I hear – and I also have ears in certain places – our queen Catherine bears it all with a patient shrug. It would be a huge relief were she to bear a child, a proper and legitimate heir to the throne. Perhaps that would encourage Charles to look no further than his own palace."

"Things have gone too far!" Fisher growled. "Puritanical laws went too far, that I freely admit. But now, the tables are turned and licentiousness rules in its stead. It is not good enough!"

"Is the country similarly disillusioned?" Forbes queried.

"Probably not," Fisher admitted. "I believe that the people as a whole are revelling in these new-found freedoms. Understandable, I suppose after so many years of repression. But I have further news to impart. What knowledge have you of this new trade being conducted between Africa, England, and the Sugar Islands?"

"I have heard nothing at all," Forbes perked up at the change of subject. "Have they discovered some new, exciting, edible commodity in Africa?"

"Hardly so," Fisher growled. "The commodity appears to be of the human variety. It seems that the Portuguese started at it some years past – taking black slaves forcibly from Africa, then shipping them as workers for the plantations. It now seems that some of our shipping traders have cottoned onto the business and are operating it themselves from Bristol and Liverpool."

"Then they must be stopped!" Forbes was horrified. "To deal with humans as if they were nothing more than goods to be bartered – that is utterly reprehensible!

"You ignore one small fact, my ecclesiastical friend. The trade is likely to reap huge profits – profits that the state needs desperately. I will wager that it will be quietly encouraged – the argument being that the commodity in question is neither Christian nor worthy of respect."

"That argument I shall never condone!" Forbes stated. "Even though not Christian, they are still a part of God's creation!"

"Never stopped us Englishmen slaughtering Muslims by the thousand during the years of the crusades!" Forbes snorted. "And that with the blessing and encouragement of the church at the time!"

CHAPTER V

It was at the end of the second week of November that Paul Larkin and Jamie eventually rode down from the moor. Their work would probably not recommence until the following Easter. Larkin himself was in two moods – one was unhappy to be leaving the wild wasteland that he had come to love and respect; the other was to relish the prospect of a comfortable bed, regular meals, and warm fires.

Jamie was simply happy that their work had yielded such a rich supply of finds. He had surprised himself that such an occupation would take as strong a hold upon him. Seventeen years old, he looked back on his previous life – playing japes upon all and sundry, dodging heavy work on the vegetable field. Am I really now growing up, he asked himself with an inwards grin.

Their horses clattered into the rear courtyard of Brimley – the young ostler running out to take their horses. Luke Farmer came hot on his heels, followed by Kit Warden and two other house servants. Quickly, the two pack horses were relieved of the large bags, the two mounts taken into the stables for grooming and feeding.

"Welcome back, Colonel," Luke smiled at his boss. "May I take it that the moor will not see you again for a while?"

"Indeed, you may," Larkin grinned at him. "We now have weeks of work to do, making proper catalogue of our finds, making good copy of the rough maps. I doubt that the moor will see us again until well into the next year!"

"Your rooms have been ready for you for some days – fires lit, bed aired, and clothes as fresh as a daisy. I have also had prepared a room for Jamie, but he shall have to collect his own spare clothes from his home."

"Then, the very first thing I require is hot water for a long and relaxing bath," Larkin made for the door into the rear hall. "Jamie

– perhaps you would like to go to your home to tell of your safe return.”

“Aye, Colonel. I shall walk there now – I have ridden more than enough for one day!”

“Twas a mere ten miles!” Larkin gaped at him. “In my days with the army, we would do thrice that every day for seven days on end!”

“And nursed your arse for as many days afterwards,” Jamie muttered to himself. Aloud, he said a brief farewell and set off to walk to his home.

Meanwhile, the many bags were carried up to the room outside Larkin’s bedroom. It was here that he would sit down with Jamie to write up reams of notes, make a fair copy on a huge parchment of the bits of the moor they had mapped.

Larkin watched as two servants lugged large buckets of hot water to fill the wooden tub. When the tub was filled, he thanked the two men, stripped off and sank gratefully into the warmth to soak off the grime and stiffness.

“Tis a good master we have,” one servant said to his mate as they arrived back in the kitchens with the empty buckets. “He actually thanked us for our work!”

Jamie was greeted with hugs from Gil and Ella as he arrived at the old, familiar kitchen.

“Back safe and sound,” his mother grinned at her full-grown son. “I suppose you will be busy with your Colonel for many weeks now.”

“In times past, he would be your knight and you his squire,” Gil ruffled his son’s hair. “Instead of which, you are his clerk and scribe. I for one would never have dreamed such an occupation for the young scallywag we used to know!”

Rosie, having been appraised of her brother’s homecoming, hurtled in from the apothecary’s and fetched a sisterly blow to Jamie’s arm.

“Ouch!” Jamie grunted. “The work you do with pestle and mortar has given you unseemly muscles for a girl.”

“Grown woman, if you please,” Rosie replied. “So, you are back for the winter!”

"Aye – and much work to do. But why has not some young man whisked you away – or are you still far too ugly to warrant the attention?"

"I am still far too busy learning my craft! Not that I want for attention, despite your repeated assertion that I am far too ugly! I favour our mama, and she is still as beautiful as ever she was!" Rosie retorted.

"Aye, you have that right," Gil planted a kiss of Ella's cheek. "Beautiful from the moment she wakes until the moment I incur her displeasure!"

"And that is never long in coming!" Ella grinned at her husband. "Now, be off with the lot of you or dinner will be delayed and cold."

Following one of his mother's rabbit stews, Jamie gathered his spare clothes into a bundle, hefted it onto his shoulder, then made his way back to Brimley and to the room that had been set aside for him. He was looking forward eagerly to making a start on the writing and cataloguing.

It was two days later that Larkin and Jamie got around to unpacking the many artifacts that they had collected. Each had a small, paper label attached by a piece of string. On the paper was the date it had been found, plus the precise location.

There were over one hundred such items, all placed in military rows upon a long trestle table that had been placed directly under the window, to catch as much light as possible. There were flint tools, a small collection of crockery pots, several very rusty knives, pieces of granite shaped into cubes, and a host of other individual items.

"I would suggest that we start by writing the diary of events," Larkin said quietly. "The items we found will trigger memories as we come to them, but we need to collate our notes into some proper chronological order."

By dinner, they had managed a mere five days, each day with its date, its precise location, and what they had (or had not) found there.

When they recommenced, Jamie made a tentative suggestion.

"Why do we not make up the large map as we go?" he asked. "Then we could make a note against each location that refers to the notes we are making."

"That, young Jamie, is an excellent notion," Larkin agreed. "We shall have to start again, each day taking us far longer than we have managed so far – but each day shall then be complete – or as complete as our rough notes and memories may achieve."

As the light was starting to fade, Luke Farmer arrived with a flagon of ale and two mugs – to tide the two men over until supper. He gazed at the array of items spread across the table. And then he did a double take.

"Pardon me interrupting, Colonel – but that old flask. May I enquire where you found it?"

"Why? Has it some significance for you?"

"Aye, Colonel – it has some significance. There is a name just about visible upon the old leather – and it is a name that I certainly recognise. It will also be recognised by Kit Warden. Also, it will be recognised by our old sergeant who lives and works at Trusham."

"Then I have to suppose that it comes from a time when you were all serving the late king in his battles against Parliament."

"Aye, Colonel, and they were times of hardship and worry."

"Could this sergeant be persuaded to come here so that all three of you could enlighten me as to this flask?"

"When he hears of it, you may be sure he will be here like a shot! I shall dispatch one of the young lads to Trusham in the morning to deliver a message."

"It would appear that you, Jamie, will be busy writing the full story of one very old, battered flask. Maybe, it shall be the best recorded of any find we have so far made!"

It was the following Sunday when Michael Brown sat in the warm study with the battered flask in his hands. Luke Farmer and Kit Warden sat next to him, whilst Larkin sat in an armchair with Jamie at his side with a stack of paper, ink and a selection of ready-sharpened quills.

"Our story," Brown cleared his throat, "begins with our mission. I led a small troop of scouts to spy on a unit of

Parliamentary soldiers that were, in their turn, spying upon the army led by Lord Wentworth. This army was encamped upon Bovey Heath, some soldiers billeted in the town itself. That were ten years ago, but that battle has never left my thoughts. Wentworth was a disaster as commander and his troops were scattered far and wide. After it was over, my small unit debated long and hard about what we should then do."

"Aye," Farmer broke in. "Some were for simply returning home. Others were for heading to Tavistock where we knew the rest of the king's army would gather – or so we thought!"

"In the end, I led the unit north so as to cross the moor," Brown started off again. "We were almost caught by a patrol but managed to evade them. And then, much later, we ascended to the moor and set off westwards. And then, as often happens, down came a thick mist. I ordered a halt as I knew that a dense mist was our sworn enemy up there. That did not sit well with one man in particular. Herrick, his name was. He managed to persuade two others to join him and to press onwards, despite not being able to see more than two paces in front of his nose."

He came to a stop at that point, searching his memory.

"You be searching for their names," Kit warden smiled. "I remember them very well as one joined us here much later. They were Porter and Andrews."

"Aye – Porter and Andrews," Brown nodded. "Herrick simply led them off despite my warnings and orders not to leave the unit. Luke and Kit can now take up the story, as they know what happened afterwards far better than I."

"We eventually got to Torrington and were a part of that dreadful day when the church exploded, killing and maiming hundreds," Farmer went on.

"I was one such – and tended afterwards with care," Brown added.

"Luke and I managed to evade discovery, then made our way over many days across the moor – where we eventually ended up here at Brimley and were taken on by the old steward," Warden carried on the narrative. "Twas some time after that we were joined by young Andrews. We knew no more until that lad developed the winter fever and was like to die. He summoned us all to his bedside, wanting to make confession. The tale he told explains the flask."

Farmer took a deep breath. "It seems that Herrick led the other two onwards and got hopelessly lost – as we had said he would. Porter, by that time, was almost frozen to death and was slowing Herrick up. According to young Andrews, Herrick simply killed Porter so as not to delay them. Andrews said that the action sickened him and, when Herrick threatened to do the same to him if he held them up, he waited until his back was turned and kicked him in the head so hard that he thought at first he had killed the man. But, feeling his neck, discovered he was just about alive, although slowly freezing. Andrews confessed to bringing about his death."

"But we found the flask deep inside a pixie hole, together with a skeleton," Jamie paused from his writing.

"Then Herrick must have recovered enough to stagger onwards, then fell into the hole and could not get out," Larkin summed up. "But you say the three of them were armed soldiers. What happened to his sword and pistol, I wonder?"

"That would have been discovered and taken long since. Some man up on the moor will have them to this day!" Warden snorted. "They shall never be found now."

"Well – and so ends the mystery of one battered old flask!" Larkin was relieved to have learned so much. It would make their find that much more interesting to those who ever bothered to read the forthcoming journal.

Adam Clements deceived his wife. Not that Nell would have minded as the deception was perfectly innocent of purpose. On the pretence of travelling to Bovey Tracey to check on the progress of a consignment of granite, he went instead to the bookseller's shop that was half-way up Bovey's main street.

Gaston Bessant was the son of Huguenot parents, both of whom had died some winters before. The family had been made welcome in Bovey Tracey, especially as they bought the bookshop previously owned by Hubert and Mercy Green – two ultra-Puritan busybodies who were not in the slightest bit missed. Gaston had married Glory Allen, daughter of Dick and Sal at the tavern. Their daughter Isobel worked tirelessly in the shop, making lists of books that they needed to buy into stock, corresponding with the many customers who wanted specific items. Isobel, eighteen years old, took after her mother – a mass of auburn curls. She had already turned down seven offers for her hand as believing the young men were hardly in her league when it came to learning. She was waiting for someone who could hold his own in debate.

She looked up from the latest list as Adam entered the shop, closing the door quietly behind him.

"A very good day to you, Master Clements," she gave him a friendly smile. "May I enquire how are Nell and little Kate?"

"Nell is as she always is – hale and healthy and busy from morn until night. Kate is now helping in the workroom – or so she claims. The two of them are almost inseparable."

"And how may I help you today?"

"That is not easy to explain," Adam admitted. "Nell has of recent times buried herself into a study of the heavens. Do you have any book that may aid her in that pursuit?"

Isobel did not hesitate for even a fraction of a second. "We have at least a dozen that may be of interest," she said. "They range from detailed explanations of the theories of Signor Galileo, the names and locations of the planets and major stars, two books by Catholic clerics that deplore such study. Plus, we have recently acquired a copy of a book that lays out the findings of Master Copernicus."

That aroused Adam's interest. "I have heard Nell mention the name Copernicus. She says the name almost in terms of reverence. May I see the book?"

It took Isobel mere minutes to locate the small book. It was exquisitely bound in maroon leather, the titles imprinted in gold on the front and spine.

"Tis written by someone who required to remain anonymous," Isobel explained. "That probably means that he is almost certainly from Rome, fearing the wrath of the Cardinals."

"I see that the writer styles himself 'Semper Veritas Laudate'," Adam note.

"That is rather bad Latin," Isobel grinned. "It means, very roughly, 'truth be praised forever'".

"Then I simply must purchase it. How much will it cost me?"

He didn't even raise an eyebrow when Isobel told him. He left the shop with the book wrapped carefully in a linen cloth. Nell would be delighted with it.

It was just past dinner when Harry Cove received a somewhat breathless visitor. Robert Hook stood in the hall with the estate's shepherd standing behind him.

"Master Bailiff," Hook was almost as breathless as the young man behind him. "Bernie has discovered a sack of valuables poked behind his hut on the twenty-acre field."

"Aye, tis as Haddock says," Bernie Wheatcroft nodded, coming into view. Hook, because of his facial similarity to a fish, had always been called Haddock.

"I do not suppose you left this sack where anyone could come to collect it?" Harry asked.

"Nay, Master Bailiff. That would be stupid to have left it. It stands just without, by the step."

Harry called for Hob who had just returned from escorting Kitty and Poppy back for afternoon lessons. Together, the four men went out to examine the sack and its contents.

Bernie and Haddock expressed no surprise as they had already seen them. But Harry and Hob whistled at the array of items that they placed on the step. Six very expensive silver candlesticks, one small coffer that was encrusted with jewels, a small leather pouch with ten gold coins, a ceremonial dagger similarly encrusted with what looked like sapphires.

"Well, there is nobody hereabouts that owned as much as that!" Hob grunted. "Either it has come from a distance, or it has been collected from many different sources." Harry turned to Bernie.

"When was the last time you ventured behind that hut?" he asked.

"Twas yesterday morning when I went to relive myself behind the hut. It were not there then! I did the same this morning and there it were. I made sure the sheep were safe in the field first before running down with it to report the finding."

Bernie had the run of six different fields where he could graze the estate's sheep. Each had a small hut where Bernie would sleep so as to be on hand if any of the animals needed his attention – or to chase off foxes if woken by his dog.

"And Rumble did not alert you to anyone coming to deposit the sack?"

"Nay – and that's the funny part. Rumble never misses anything!"

"Tis possible the dog recognised whoever it was," Hook offered.

Harry knew what had to be done. He collected all the items and stuffed them back into the sack, took the sack indoors and locked it securely into the estate safe room.

"Go and get Sam Garvey. We must get up there to see what clues may be found," he told Hook. Hook and Garvey, in years gone by, had been expert trackers when in the Parliamentary army.

It was well over an hour later when Harry, Hob, Garvey and Hook stood behind the hut. It was close by the northern end of the field, sheltered by a large stand of trees. Garvey and Hook immediately started casting about for signs of disturbance. Harry and Hob left them to it, watching Bernie and Rumble gather the flock to move it to the next field.

"Rained last night, Master Bailiff," Sam Garvey came back having left Hook in the trees. "Good luck for us and poor luck for Mister Thief. We've found a small trail leading from the hut through the trees. Haddock be following it now if you want to join us."

They followed Garvey into the trees. They noted that Garvey kept well to one side of the track they were following. Just at the point where the trees came to an end, Hook was standing and casting about.

"Bugger came over this rocky bit. Sam and I will have to cover it all to see where it may lead at the other side of the patch."

It was Garvey who gave a shout. "Found it – goes across this grassy bit to those few trees yonder."

Now well to the north of the river Bovey, the four followed the indistinct tracks to the trees. It was there that Hook gave a loud curse.

"Sod and buggery! Bastard left his horse here, went back to it and rode off just west of north. Lustleigh lies there!"

Harry and Hob took his word for it. They would not have spotted the tracks in the first place.

"My jurisdiction does not carry that far!" Harry snorted. "All we can do is ride out tomorrow and ask around. We cannot demand."

Hob's ears pricked up at that. He loved nothing more than riding hither and yon. A ride up to Lustleigh and beyond suited him very well indeed.

CHAPTER VI

Adam Clements was just on the point of leaving his desk when there came a knock at the front door. He heard the usual scampering feet as young Lottie rushed down the stairs to answer it. A few minutes later, his office door opened, and the young servant girl poked her head around.

"Master Adam, tis Master Hawk and a young seaman to speak to you."

Rufus Hawk was one of the captains of his three ships that plied between South Devon and wherever the cargo of granite was needed. Adam had spoken to Hawk only that morning when the cog had berthed to await its next cargo. Hawk ushered a young deckhand in front of him and shook Adam's hand.

"And who may this be – tis certainly not one of our crews," Adam gave the young fellow a puzzled look.

"Nay, Master Adam. Tis Tam Blower – and tis right that you hear his story for yourself. I know twill be of concern to you and to Mistress Nell."

"Then come in and sit. I shall call Nell here so that we may both hear this tale. No, on second thoughts, come up above so that we may all sit in comfort. This office is not designed for comfort!"

He led the way up the stairs to the large parlour where a fire was burning and there were seats aplenty. Nell, finished her work for the day, was playing with little Kate and the new kitten that had miraculously appeared at their door the previous day. Nell looked up and gave the ship's master a friendly smile.

"Master Hawk, I bid you good day," she said, passing Kate and the kitten to Lottie. "Pray sit and refresh yourself with a mug of ale."

"Thankee kindly, Mistress. But I believe that you and Master Adam first need to hear the tale that this young man has to tell. I know that it will be of mighty concern to you both."

"Apparently, this young fellow is named Tam Blower – and so far, this all I know of him," Adam told his wife.

"Tam – start your story as you told it to me. And be sure it is complete in every detail!" Hawk ordered.

"Aye, Master," Tam cleared his throat. "I am from London docks. My mother and father are still there, my father being a wharf-hand. From the age of twelve, I went on little voyages with whatever cog needed a deck boy. I sailed to Hull mainly with a trading vessel. Then just over one year past, I sailed on another old cog to Liverpool where I was accosted by a bosun off an ocean-going cog. He told me that they needed a young lad to fill out the crew for a long voyage. He paid me some coin in advance. Well, seemed too good an opportunity to miss, so I left word with my old master to get the message to my folks and joined the cog. Twas named Flying Angel – and nothing less like an angel it turned out to be! We loaded many crates that were stuffed with cheap trinkets made of tin and glass beads – poor stuff made to look like jewels. Some crates were filled with old pistols. I have fired a pistol once and knew that any one of these would as like blow the hand off the user as wound an enemy! Still, was no concern of mine if we were taking these goods to folk who should know better. We sailed on the next morning tide – and a long journey it proved to be. We sailed all the way down England, rounded the tip of Cornwall and set off south. I asked my deck mates where we were bound and was scared when they said twas the Africa coast. I had never before sailed so far."

He paused for a draught of ale before continuing. Adam had a worrying thought that he knew already where this tale was heading.

"On the way, we put into Lisbon for fresh food and to fill the water butts. Then we were off again, again due south. My mates told me of the coasts that we passed. First was Morocco, then we hugged the coast as near as we dared until, some weeks later, we put into a small port where the smells of Africa hit me for the first time – and I hope, the last! Twas the heat, the spices, the baking earth. As we tied up at the berth, a large man came aboard and supervised the unloading of our cargo. That took two whole days. Where it went, I have no knowledge. And then we were all set to making the cargo hold into summat different. Planks were laid fore and aft, close packed and in three layers deep. I nearly dropped at the sight of our new cargo – lines of black men all chained together in long lines. Most were young men, but there were also some boys. I watched as they were led below and laid down packed like fish in a barrel on the planking."

Tam grasped his mug and took a deep swallow of ale, then continued his story as Adam and Nell sat in silence.

"One of my jobs was to take bread and water down to the hold twice a day. The stink was about too much for me and I were sick the first times I had that duty. There were three of us set to that task. I managed to find out from one of the older hands that we would then cross the wide ocean to the sugar islands, where the slaves would be unloaded and sold at a market. The man told me that he had watched this market once before. Twas attended by the plantation masters. They would inspect the black men, even opening their mouths to count their teeth. The fittest fetched the highest prices. Where the coin from the sales went, he had no idea. Anyway, we were far from the islands when the first of the slaves were found dead. Master told everyone to wait until we had a batch of the dead and then they would be disposed overboard. And that is what happened. Five times on that voyage, we brought up groups of dead and simply tossed them overboard. Master said that the owner would be paid compensation for loss of goods!"

"And that is what he said, loss of goods?" Nell was almost too shocked to speak.

"Aye, mistress – loss of goods. It seemed years but were about six weeks later that we docked in in the islands. The remaining slaves were herded ashore to be sold next day at market. I counted how many were lost on that voyage – twere sixty-eight. Us crew were then given the task of cleaning the hold – and a worse job I hope never to have to do again in my lifetime! It were like emptying the deepest cesspit, and we all jumped into the sea afterwards to wash off the stink. When master were satisfied, we loaded our new cargo – sugar and some fruits I had never seen before. Also, there were bales of tobacco leaves. We set sail the next day to return to Liverpool, but I never reached there. We put into Cork weeks later to get provisions, and twas there I jumped ship. No way on this good earth I was going to do that voyage again. I hid for a few days and saw my ship sail off up the coast back to Liverpool. Some days later, I managed to get a ship bound for Plymouth – and twas there I found Master Hawk who said he would take me here to tell my story.”

Adam and Nell sat as if stupefied as the story ended. Hawk, who had heard it before, waited quietly. Eventually, Adam could hold the silence no longer.

“One question, Tam – did you ever find out the name of the owner of the vessel?”

“Oh, aye, that I did. The senior deckhand got to talking one night when we were becalmed for a day in mid-ocean. He said that Flying Angel and five other cogs were owned by a Lord Longthorpe – or that was the name I think he said. All were called Flying something or other and all were plying this trade.”

“Then he is making a fortune. I wonder how many more there are like him?” Adam thought aloud.

“That is the most horrible tale I have ever heard,” Nell was looking as if she might be sick. “We go to Bovey on the morrow. We must relate what we have heard.”

“One point, master,” Hawk said to Adam. “Young Tam has proved himself a good seaman on our short trip from Plymouth. I can offer him a berth if you are willing.”

“Aye – and nobody deserves it better! But our cargo is Granite blocks and tis very heavy work!”

“Master, I care not if cargo be snakes or toads! Anything would be heaven compared to what I had to do. I thank you and Master Hawk. I shall be your very best deckhand.”

Later that evening, with Kate and young Lottie asleep, Adam at last presented his present to Nell.

Nell unfolded the linen wrapping and gave a gasp of sheer delight as the book came to light. She handled it almost reverently.

“I do not know how to express my thanks for this, Adam,” she said quietly. “A simple ‘thank-you’ seems totally inadequate. It shall be my most treasured possession – after you and Kate, of course.”

"Aye, I thought you would like it," Adam grinned. "Isobel Bessant sold it to me last time I were in Bovey. Knowing your interest in the heavens, I knew at once it were the book for you."

"I shall read it carefully. Just maybe it may alter some of what I have written. I need to speak to Mary about it all as she is the one to make sense of it all."

"I know you have penned many pages on your thoughts. I am not exactly stupid, you know! Why not read it to me and I shall listen to your thoughts."

"I shall do that with great pleasure." Nell hugged her husband. Not for the first time she thanked also her lucky stars for his care and consideration. Not all were so lucky!

CHAPTER VII

Just over one week later, and with November coming to its gloomy end, Harry and Hob held a conference with Reverend James Forbes. On the table before them were the items from the sack.

"There is absolutely no reference to a church amongst these items," Forbes said with assurance. "The candlesticks could of course come from a church but are more likely to come from a large house. To connect them to a church's silverware, there would be a pyx, a ciborium, a crucifix or similar items. When you add this very elaborate small coffer, the gold coins, and the jewel encrusted dagger, the likelihood becomes even greater that they are the property of some very rich family."

"Aye, that was our thought as well," Harry nodded. "Hob has had the time of his life visiting every rich household for miles around. He did not say what the items were, simply that some very valuable items had been found. If anyone could list them, then that would be the owner."

"First, I went north where the trackers said the hoofprints pointed. Nobody in Lustleigh reported any theft. I even went as far as Moretonhampstead, Christow, and Chudleigh – with similar results," Hob said.

"I have sent messages to Ashburton, Newton, Totnes, Coombe, Stoke, and a whole host of other places. So far, there have been no replies. Tis a complete mystery!" Harry reported.

"And there is no mark on any of the items that may identify their source?" Forbes asked.

"None that we can see. But I had an idea to ask Rosie to make drawings of the pieces so that these could be posted around the towns and villages."

"That would be a very good idea. That young lady has a wonderful gift. Many folks hereabouts have pictures that she has drawn – and all are lifelike!"

Hob sat and cogitated before saying what he thought was obvious. "But none of this explains why someone should ride south to Parke, walk a bit further with a sack of valuable items, deposit it behind a shepherd's hut, and then disappear again whence he had come!"

"As I said, tis a mystery that we may never solve," Harry grunted.

On the way back to Parke, the two called in at the apothecary to speak to Rosie. She readily agreed to come to the estate and to make drawings of the items. She was as intrigued as the rest of the small town.

She spoke to James and Avril who said that she must go and do what she could. Riding pillion behind Harry, a satchel of drawing materials over her shoulder, she was soon seated at the large table looking with some awe at the silver and jewels that glinted in the candlelight.

She reached out to the exquisite, small coffer and turned it over in her hands.

"It is chased with silverwork, covered in small jewels that look to me to be real and not glass. The wood is something I have never seen before. Tis not oak or walnut as one might expect but has a dark red hue and fine black lines. I wonder what it is."

Hob, who prided himself on a knowledge of woods, added that it was a hardwood and not anything grown in England – like oak or ash.

Rosie replaced the little coffer and picked up one of the candlesticks.

"The chasing in the silver up the stem is very fine," she observed. "The base is very heavy and is probably filled with lead to make it stable. The underside of the base has scratchings that may have been made by its being sat upon a stone shelf. No – these scratchings have a definite pattern. All are straight lines and not a curve amongst them."

She took a stick of charcoal that had been sharpened to a fine point and made a much larger copy of the markings upon a piece of paper.

/ / F / / appeared in large format.

"That just *might* be the mark of the silversmith who made it," she observed.

"Then Hob is on his travels again," Harry grinned at his young deputy. "There is a silversmith in Newton to visit first. There is another in Ashburton."

"But there is snow coming," Hob objected.

"Then all the more need for warm clothing and a good quality waterproof cape!" Harry laughed.

Hob took Rosie safely back to Gil and Ella. She told her parents what she had been doing and the discovery she had made.

"You may have found the very first clue to where they came from," Ella said, looking proudly at a daughter who never ceased to amaze her.

On the Sunday, Adam, Nell, and Kate rode through light snow to Bovey Tracey. The three, together with Lottie, had attended an early service, then sent Lottie off to spend the rest of the day with the friend she had found in a nearby house. Avril had also invited Rosie and her family to dinner – a joint of mutton was already turning on the kitchen spit.

The first thing that Nell did when arriving was to creep quietly into the kitchen for a hug with the woman she had always regarded as her surrogate mother. Avril returned the hug, then looked at the flushed face of her adopted daughter.

"Are you?" she asked.

She received a happy nod in return. "I told Adam but yesterday when I was absolutely sure. The child will be born towards the end of next June – maybe in very early July. Kate is yet to be told, so I need to pick the right moment. Lottie will be very excited with yet another little one to spoil!"

She helped Avril serve the dinner of roast mutton, roasted vegetables and Avril's own special sauce made from mint, rosemary, meat juices, and honey. Conversation ceased as it was all eaten in an almost reverent silence.

"Yummy, yummy," was Kate's verdict as she scraped the last vestige of the sauce onto a piece of bread.

"Aye – that was absolutely delicious," Ella remarked, just stopping Jamie as he reached for a scrap of crackling on the serving platter.

"You said that you had somewhat disturbing news for us," James reminded Adam.

"Aye – disturbing is almost too weak a word to describe it," Adam replied. "It concerns a young lad that one of my ships' masters brought with him when he returned from his last trip. The lad's name is Tam Blower and the tale he related is something I had heard vague rumours of but had never before credited."

He then held them spellbound as he went through Tam's story in detail. Through it all, Rosie turned pale – exactly as Nell had done when she had sat through it. Avril and Ella were close to tears when Adam at last came to the end.

"Dear God in heaven!" James was the first to react. "That is truly wicked. How can anyone regard people as of such little account that they be transported hundreds of miles from their home, sold into slavery, and all in the name of trade?"

Gil, who was perhaps the most worldly-wise of all present, gave a shrug. He looked to Adam for support.

"'Tis simple, I'm afraid," he spoke quietly. "Many would regard these people as black heathens, a very inferior part of God's creation. Those same people will see nothing amiss in using them as a trading commodity."

"Aye, Gil has that right," Adam nodded. "Tam said that the master of the ship, plus the majority of his crew, saw nothing wrong in disposing of the dead – they were simply a trading loss that had to be borne!"

James had been deep in thought. "I am willing to wager that the Church would see nothing amiss in it either. They would regard it as an opportunity to bring the heathens to an understanding of the Christian faith – in fact, doing the black people a great service by bringing them into the light. Do not be in any doubt that the authorities will smile with delight when the revenue from taxation of the profits start to pour into the coffers!"

"That is an utterly cynical view," Rosie objected.

"Aye, I know. But it is not my view! I abhor the trade as much as anyone here, but the country's wealth will undoubtedly be enhanced significantly by it!"

"That will almost certainly be the case," Adam and Gil both nodded in agreement. "There will be no stopping it, no matter how many believe it disgraceful."

Litle Kate had been listening to all that had passed between the adults. "Do they take the little children as well?" she asked.

"Nay – they would not be so wicked as to take little ones away from their families!" Nell hastened to comfort her little daughter. Adam gave her a smile of agreement, well knowing as did Nell that the direct opposite was true.

To drag Kate's concerns away from the subject, Nell decided that it was now an excellent opportunity to tell her daughter that she would soon have a playmate.

"How would you like it if you had a little brother or sister?" she asked.

"Oh, wow, mama – really?"

"Aye – by next summer you will have a baby to help me with, to teach how to walk and to play!"

Kate leapt down from her high stool and ran to her mother as the rest of the table erupted in laughter and congratulations.

"I'll be a big sister!" Kate crowed.

Only a light dusting of snow covered the road between Bovey Tracey and Newton Abbot as Hob, muffled up in layers of wool, trotted his mount carefully towards the larger town. The Monday had dawned with bright sunshine, a bitterly cold wind, and clear skies. Hob just knew that more snow was on the way!

Tucked into his pouch was the drawing of the marks from the base of one candlestick. However, he had not the faintest idea where in the town he would find the silversmith, only that he knew for certain that there was one. Being wise in the ways of towns and villages, he made straight for the nearest tavern. A tavern master knew everybody!

"Aye, tis down the left of Courtney Street, about four doors before St. Lawrence church, he was told as he downed a mug of warmed ale. "You may walk there in just a few minutes."

Leaving his horse in the tavern's stables to be brushed and fed, Hob walked down the street, looking with interest at the shops as he passed. He also noted with approval the state of the street itself. The good citizens had swept the remaining snow into tidy piles, ensuring safe passage for the shoppers. He came to the silversmith's shop and went in.

"A good morning to you, young master. What is it you seek? A present for the lady wife?" asked a tall, spindly man wearing a leather apron the like of which was new to Hob in that it had a large, gaping pouch at the front.

"Nay, nothing but information, I am afraid," Hob answered, glancing at the array of silver and gold items on display. "I come from Bovey seeking advice."

He took out the drawing and laid it on the counter.

"Have you seen the like of this afore?"

The man reached for a pair of thick glasses and set them perched upon his bony nose.

"Oh, aye – I am well acquainted with this mark," he nodded. "Tis the mark of Lionel Fetters. He is silversmith down in Totnes. Where did you obtain this mark?"

"I am deputy Bailiff in Bovey," Hob explained. "This is a mark found upon the base of a lot of items found abandoned on the Parke estate. We need to know who is the owner - and this is our only clue."

"Then a rather longer journey awaits you," the man retorted. "And unless I am mistaken, one taken in more snow!"

"Aye, you have that right!" Hob grunted. His eye was taken by a small brooch with an equally small amethyst set in its centre. "How much would that cost me?"

The man named a price that had Hob a trifle shaken. But it was rather lovely and he knew that May would love it. He countered with an offer below that asked by the shopkeeper. They settled somewhere in the middle. Hob placed it wrapped in a piece of linen back into his pouch along with the drawing, bade good day to the silversmith, and retraced his footsteps to the tavern for his dinner.

"Off to Totnes, then!" Harry grinned at his deputy later that afternoon.

"Aye, but not in deep snow!" Hob countered.

CHAPTER VIII

The umpteenth meeting of The Sane and Sensible differed from all its predecessors in that violent disagreement was the order of the day. On one side was Reverend James Forbes, puce with rage and joined by Matthew Kent – not quite as furious as Forbes. On the other was Colonel Fisher – equally bellowing his counter arguments; whilst Paul Larkin hovered uncertainly between the two.

"Damned black heathens deserve to be dragged into the pure light of God's grace – surely you can see that!" Fisher growled.

"What I see is a desecration of God's good order of things!" Forbes growled back. "If He in His wisdom had wanted the black races made cognisant of His Son's saving grace, He would have chosen to do so in His own time – not as a means of making filthy profits!"

"That makes far more sense to me than does the unscrupulous money-making by traders who see nothing beyond an extension of trade," Kent nodded towards the Reverend.

Larkin was not at all comfortable with either view. On the one hand, he saw the righteousness of spreading the message of Christ to heathens. But on the other hand, was it right to do so in the name of trade? He was used to taking problems home and thinking them through at leisure, not having to declare precipitously in public. He had always been a careful and thoughtful commander.

Fisher raised yet another point. "The Court and many members of the Lords already have black servants – dressed as civilised human beings, not as damned savages in loincloths. They are serving the gentry as befits their station -and being taught Godly ways in the process!"

"And that makes it correct, does it?" Forbes shouted back. "Snatch them from their families, drag them miles across the ocean, change them into liveried servants, whip them for disobedience or for not understanding? Tis a backward step to the times of the Romans and their evil practice of slavery!"

Larkin had heard enough to want this 'debate' to end so that he could mull things over quietly. He wanted to reach some middle ground.

"Colonel – can you agree that the black heathens are indeed a part of God's creation?" he asked, appealing for quiet reason.

"Oh, aye – they are indeed – and put there for us to drag out of their ignorance!" Fisher snorted.

"And where in Holy Scripture does it say that we have that duty and obligation?" Kent asked.

"Go forth and take this message to the world! That's where!"

"And would you, were you a younger man, go to Africa and partake of the enforced taking of these people?" Kent persisted.

"Aye, without a second's hesitation!"

"And pocket the profits without the slightest qualm?" Forbes probed.

"And why should not my honest endeavours be rewarded? I served my generals, killed and took prisoners for ransom when they told me to – and I got paid for doing so. Where is the difference, pray?"

"If you cannot see the difference, then this argument becomes an exercise in utter futility!" Forbes snorted.

The meeting, for the first time ever, broke up in discord. Nobody doubted that, when the next meeting occurred, it would be as if a new page had been turned. Kent rode back to Brimley still wondering at the intransigence of the old colonel. Larkin rode home convinced that he needed to use pen and paper to list the pros and cons. He was ever a careful man.

A few sunny days during the second week of December had banished the small amounts of snow. All that remained were the occasional puddles of water on the otherwise well-maintained roads. Hob set out after breakfast riding his favourite horse. He would cover the seventeen miles to Totnes in two hours if he trotted, then cantered, and allowed the occasional gallop.

He had decided upon the 'northern' route – through Ashburton and on towards Buckfastleigh, where he would turn south towards Dartington and then Totnes. He had never been to Totnes before. Stopping abruptly at the top of the main street, he looked askance at the steep hill that went down through the town.

"Aye – tis steep!" a passing fellow remarked with a broad grin. "New to Totnes then?"

"Aye, never been here afore," Hob answered. "I'm after a silversmith named Fetters. Have you a notion where he may be found?"

"Old Grumblepot? Oh, aye – everybody hereabouts knows old Grumblepot Fetters. Miserable bugger! His shop is down there, past the bridge, then three doors on the right. His prices are not for the likes of me!"

"I do not fancy riding down these steep cobbles," Hob eyed the hill with some misgiving.

"You shall not have to. Walk the horse down and you'll find stabling on your left at Guildhall Yard. Then just carry on walking downwards, under the bridge and you're there."

Half an hour later, Hob opened the door to the silversmith's shop and paused in amazement as he viewed what seemed to him to be a treasure trove of silverware. A young chap behind the counter looked Hob up and down, obviously assessing the size of the purse that had just entered. He gave a grunt of disapproval.

"Aye – I am not here to purchase – as I believe you have already assessed," Hob grinned. "I am from Bovey Tracey and have need to speak with Master Fetters."

"Master be not here – he's away at Stoke Gabriel for the day."

"Then I shall have to ask you what I would have asked him," Hob took the drawing out of his pouch and laid it on the counter.

"That is master's mark," the young man exclaimed.

"So I was already told. So, he puts his mark on every piece he makes?"

"Aye, well – mostly he does. Where have you found this mark?"

Hob explained all about the finding of the sack and listed the pieces that it had contained.

"Six candlesticks," muttered the young journeyman. "Can you describe height and any other markings?"

Hob raised his hand above the counter. "About one foot and a half in height and the stems were chased in what looked like climbing ivy."

"Lady Groombridge," the journeyman nodded. "Those were made special to her order some three months past."

"And did you sell her more than the sticks?"

"Nay – twere all that were ordered."

"And where may I find this Lady – or is it a trade secret?"

"She holds a manor at Rattery – and not the easiest Lady to converse with – as I have no doubt you have been told about my master!"

"Aye – I heard something of that nature," Hob grinned. "I thank you for your time. I must be on my way back now."

Hob trudged back up the hill, pausing to look aloft at the bridge that spanned the street. He collected a well-rested horse and walked back to the top of the hill, passing the castle on his right. He stopped for a late dinner at a tavern in Buckfastleigh, then rode back to Bovey Tracey to report his findings to Harry.

Rosie arrived at Parke just as the sun was disappearing. It would be a cold and clear evening and night. The walk had taken her only a short while, but she was anxious for Mary's opinion – had been for some considerable time.

Mary, now thirty-four years old, had somehow managed to retain her looks and figure despite both the passing of the years and bearing the twins and a daughter. She was regarded as the first port of call for any in the town who needed advice or clarification of any problem. Hence, Rosie's need for a friendly consultation. Mary led her into a back room where a fire was burning, and the chairs were comfortable. Providing mulled wine and cake, she looked at her young visitor with the expectation of hearing about some young man about whom Rosie sought information.

"Well – who is it?" she asked.

"Who is who?" Rosie replied, perplexed. Then realisation dawned and she laughed. "Nay – tis not some young man. I need you to listen to some thoughts about a small book I intend to write."

Mary sat back a tad disappointed; it was high time in her opinion that Rosie settled down into marriage. She was nineteen and a very pretty young woman.

"What my thoughts entail may be regarded by some as heresy," Rosie started. "I cannot think that they are, but some well might. It concerns this earth and the heavens – and the way God created it all."

"I'm sure you are not the first person to entertain such thoughts – and you will certainly not be the last," Mary replied. "The subject has already been explored by such as Copernicus, Galileo, even Luther had some misgivings!"

"I have the gravest misgivings with the first Book of all – Genesis," Rosie began again. "For a start, it says that God took a rib from Adam and from it, created Eve. That is utter nonsense – men and women have an equal number of ribs. Any student of medicine would know that. Then there is the question of the apple and the serpent. If men are supposed to be superior in brain matter than are women, why was Eve able to convince Adam to eat the apple when he had been specifically told not to? And then comes the biggest question of all. They bore two children – Cain and Abel. Cain killed Abel. Where, pray, did the next generation come from? Did God create other beings? If so, why does it not say so? If he did not, then Abel would not have been able to father the next generation – and God's greatest creation would have come to naught. It makes no sense whatsoever!"

"Have you come to the conclusion that the story of the creation is merely that – a story?"

"Logic dictates that it must be so!" Rosie replied very firmly.

"The problem with that is this," Mary thought aloud. "If you raised these thoughts with any theologian, he would simply reply that the manner of God's works is beyond human understanding – and that we must all accept that we may *never* understand."

"Aye, I know!" Rosie groaned. "But I need to understand! I need to make sense of this world and my part in it. And that brings me to another thought. If God created this earth and all its manifold wonders, why could He not have created another? Why could there not be such as us and our plants and animals on one of the planets?"

"Why not, indeed," Mary nodded. "But you have to be very careful with whom you share these thoughts and doubts. It has been firmly established that this earth is *not* the centre of the universe. We revolve around the sun and our moon revolves around us. But all in the Church of Rome, and many of our own faith, still refuse to acknowledge that discovery. You could be heaping a store of trouble for yourself by making your views known!"

"I am truly aware of this," Rosie acknowledged. "That is why I first came to you. I *shall* put my thoughts down on paper – but not yet. I may well need years more thought before I feel capable of expressing them in a coherent manner."

Mary gave a sigh of relief. And then expounded one of her own thoughts.

"The biblical scholars state very firmly that the earth and its inhabitants was created about four thousand years ago. But very learned men of science have shown that there are rocks that must be *millions* of years old. And that the coal we burn is the result of trees and suchlike being compressed underground for many thousands of years before the supposed creation."

"Then, the story told in Genesis *must* be no more than the workings of some deluded mind!"

"Or the sincere belief in the power of God!" Mary reminded her.

Rosie, on her short way back home, was glad that she had shared her thoughts with Mary. But she was more confused than ever.

It was later that evening before Hob had a chance to report his findings to Harry. Mary, having made sure that young Lauren had said her prayers before curling up into her bed, and that the twins were engaged upon some useful (educational) pursuit, had come back downstairs to join her husband in front of the fire.

"Lady Groombridge?" Harry said, having heard Hob's story through. "I have never heard of her!"

"You may not have, but I know of a man who has," Mary said, a vague recollection of a past conversation nudging into her conscious mind.

"And which of your illustrious acquaintances would that be?" Harry gave his wife a playful poke in the ribs.

"You know him as well as I," Mary poked back. "Matthew Kent spoke her name some weeks ago when we were discussing possible donors to the school."

"Then I shall have to invite him to join me when I go to speak to this mysterious lady. Hob simply cannot go – cannot have a mere deputy calling upon the nobility!"

Hob, who knew that the remark was said in mere jest, poked out his tongue at his boss, thereby earning him a cuff about the head from his own wife. Hob made a grab for May who fled screaming in mock terror as Hob pursued her out of the parlour.

CHAPTER IX

Colonel Fisher sat nursing a glass of wine, his feet stretched towards the logs burning and crackling in the grate. Reverend James Forbes sat on the other side of the grate. Both elderly men looked at peace with the world – and not one word about their previous, somewhat heated, disagreement.

This meeting was taking place in Fisher's cottage rather than in the Bovey rectory. Forbes had fancied a ride out in the cold winter sunshine.

"Has anyone yet probed deeply into the background of this Pretty, Witty Nell?" Forbes asked.

"Not as far as I am aware. She seems to have arrived on the London scene some few years past and was taken on first as an orange seller at the theatres. Now apparently, she is a valued member of the acting company. She also favours the name Nell rather than Eleanor. From all the accounts I have received, she is an actress of some ability. She is also a woman of some beauty – or so my informants say. Our king is seemingly besotted with her – much to the annoyance of Barbara Villiers. There is little love lost betwixt the two of them!"

"And yet no sign of a legitimate heir to the throne?"

"Apparently not. By all accounts, Charles is not absent from his wife's bed more than three times per week. Poor Catherine seems destined to be a queen in all but a crown - and uncomplaining at her husband's frequent infidelities."

"And is the Court still a place of debauchery?"

"Oh aye – debauchery, infidelities galore, and seemingly nobody to keep order. Charles is certainly not the one to curtail others' so-called pleasures!"

"And what of sound government?"

"As far as my informants observe, the sounds from parliament are deafening in their silence! Sooner or later, someone will have the nerve to raise objections. But who it will be, or even when, is beyond me."

Lady Sybil Groombridge was not a happy person. Never the most even-tempered of women, she was seething with anger, causing everyone from steward down to the lowliest kitchen maid to tread very warily around her. And, she reasoned, her anger was more than justified. Someone had entered her large house, stolen six newly acquired candlesticks, and had made off with them – and nobody in the large house or on the estate being any the wiser. Lady Sybil was not a happy person.

Married at her father's insistence at the tender age of fifteen to Sir Reginald Groombridge, she had been widowed for the last nine years. She had always consoled herself that her husband, twenty-seven years her senior, would predecease her – hopefully by some considerable margin. Her dowry on marriage had been the small estate outside the little village of Rattery. Now a widow of fifty-one summers, she had sole and legal possession of that dowry – and she intended to keep it by never marrying again.

Those candlesticks, exquisitely crafted by Master Fetters, had been intended as a present to the queen. She had met Catherine of Braganza just once prior to the marriage to Charles II – and had rightly forecast a troubled union between the two. The candlesticks were intended to bring some small solace into that Lady's life. And now, some wretched thief had deprived her of the intended gift.

There came a timid knock at the door of her writing room where she had been penning a letter to her sister in far-away London. The door opened the merest crack, just wide enough for her steward to poke a scrawny neck around it.

"My Lady, there are two persons come to speak with you," the voice croaked – fully expecting to have an inkpot hurled in his direction.

"Two persons? What manner of persons?"

"One is a gentleman named Kent and the other is the Bailiff from Parke, My Lady."

"Then show them into the parlour and provide them with refreshments. Tell them I shall join them in minutes!"

The head withdrew and steps were heard shuffling along the corridor and down the stairs. Sybil finished her letter with a flourish of signature, put her pen carefully into its holder, stood and, straightening her gown, went down to see these two persons.

The slightly shorter of her two visitors effected introductions.

"Lady Groombridge, my name is Harry Cove, Bailiff of Parke. My companion is Master Kent. We are here to ask whether you have mislaid any property recently."

"Mislaid, young man is not the word I would use! Deprived of, purloined from – those are the words I would use. Property has certainly been stolen. Why? Have you news of them?"

"If I could ask you to look at a drawing, you may be able to identify the items in question," Harry drew out the picture and handed it to Sybil.

Sybil took only a moment to identify the candlestick. "I ordered a set of six of these from Fetters. They have the identical markings upon the stems that I ordered. The six were stolen from my house only ten days ago. I must assume that, as you have a drawing of them, that you had it made from one of the originals – and that you know where they are."

"Indeed so, My Lady. They are at present in the strong room at Parke."

"Then please sit and regale me with how they came to be there."

Harry went through the story of the shepherd finding the sack, the trail followed, then the discovery of the silversmith.

"I have no knowledge of any of the other items, although I could be sorely tempted to claim ownership of the purse of gold. But you bring me the best news I have received since the death of my husband! You shall stay and enjoy dinner at my table."

Having rung a bell and ordered two more places set at table, she turned her attention again to her visitors.

"You are Matthew Kent, are you not? I never forget a name or a face. I saw you on more than one occasion lurking in the corridors in Westminster."

"Aye, My Lady – you well might have done. I was for some time a peripatetic agent for Master Secretary. Your late husband was a frequent visitor to those corridors."

"Indeed, he was. Lurking and seeking favour like some damned lickspittle. I referred to him then, and still do, as a useless fart!"

"But such an anal ejaculation *does* have its uses, My Lady. It relieves pressure upon the bowels!"

Lady Sybil Groombridge threw back her head and emitted a bellow of laughter.

"Then I shall have to find another description for him," she chortled. "But you are from near Brimley, I understand."

"Indeed, I am. I bought a fine cottage following the sad departure of another great Lady – Violette Charlton."

"Aye, Violette. A great Lady as you say. But one blessed with a happy but short marriage - unlike me. Blessedly short, but miserably unhappy."

Having found the owner of some of the pieces, the two left after a splendid dinner. Harry arranged to have the candlesticks delivered in the near future.

"Now all we have to do is to find the owners of the other pieces," Harry grunted as they rode side by side back to Parke.

"Not forgetting that you are also responsible for finding the thief!" Kent gave him a broad grin.

CHAPTER X

The following morning brought another change in the weather. Down from the moor came rain clouds that quickly turned into downpours of freezing hailstones. The courtyard behind the Parke mansion was not a place to cross as the hailstones, some as large as small pebbles, bounced off the cobbles in all directions. One of the scullery maids ran back into the kitchen with her face marked with small bruises. The lower floor of the large house was deafened by her wails as Grace Barton, wife of the steward, attempted to sooth her with salves from her large supply.

In the main hall, on the first floor, Harry was attempting to hold what he termed a council of war. He had summoned what he considered to be the best brains available. James, Avril, and Mary were sat on one side of the large table whilst Harry, Hob and Matthew Kent sat facing them.

Harry outlined for all concerned the details of the problem that he had so far established. The sack, its location when deposited, the contents, the tracing of the feet and horse imprints, the discovery of one owner of the pieces.

"And how in the name of all that is holy am I supposed to proceed from here?" he asked.

"You still have to trace the owners of a very elaborate, sheathed dagger, a purse of gold coins, and a small coffer that is worth a small fortune," James noted. "May we see these items?"

Harry tossed a large key to Hob, who went to the door of the strong room and returned with the sack. He placed all the items, including the candlesticks, on the table.

Avril immediately went for the little coffer, picked it up and gazed at the jewel-encrusted surface. "The wood is rosewood and is rare indeed. As far as I am able to see, the jewels are all very real." She opened the lid and peered into the box. One hand went inside the seemingly empty interior and felt around with her fingertips. Putting the opened coffer down on the table again, she peered closely at it.

"Have you noticed that the back piece is thicker that either the front or the two sides?" she asked. "Is it possible that there is a compartment concealed in that back piece?"

"And if so, how may it be accessed," James picked up the box and fished out a small glass from his pocket. "There is the slightest indentation at the right side – ah – there we go!"

He removed half of the back panel and peered into the tiny cavity that was then exposed. "Damnation – empty!" he growled.

"Nothing within - but writing on the inner side of the false wall," Mary observed.

"Angus Templeton – 1505," James reported. "Simply scratched into the wood."

"Heavens – that is in the reign of the seventh Henry," Mary enlightened them. "And four years before that monster son of his gained the throne."

"So, are you saying that the box is at least one hundred and sixty-one years old?" Hob had used many fingers to work it out.

"Aye – that is what it says," Mary nodded.

Up until then, Kent had remained silent. "There was a family named Templeton that was associated with the eighth Henry's sister Margaret when she married the Scots king – the one they called the fourth James."

"And the grandson of that marriage became our own first James – and the Scots' sixth of that name" Mary added.

"That is all well and good," Harry grimaced at the history lesson. "But it gets us no nearer to finding the *current* owner of the box! It may well have passed through many hands in the intervening years."

"May I remind my revered husband that there may well be reference to the Templeton family somewhere in the piles of books at our own booksellers?" Mary gave him a grin.

"And I still have many contacts in Westminster," Kent added. "I shall pen a letter asking for any information that may be lurking there. It can go with the next messenger."

"And I shall spend a few happy hours with Isobel at the bookshop," Mary was delighted at the prospect.

"But what about the dagger and the coins?" Hob put a damper on proceedings.

"The ownership of coins cannot be established. The dagger is yet another matter that we need to pursue," Harry retorted.

"And we are still no nearer finding this mysterious thief!" Hob was determined to have the last word.

Since returning from the moor, Jamie had spent most of his time helping his parents with the smallholding – mainly getting it ready for the early spring planting. But he spent the remainder of his time at Brimley making detailed lists of all the items they had found and writing up a fair copy of their journal.

On that gloomy afternoon, he opened the final little sack of finds. He laid out three old knives, one item which looked like a very crude iron chisel, and a small screw of waterproofed canvas.

Expecting to find it was just that, he unwrapped it and sat back somewhat amazed as a very small object was revealed. It was in the form of a sort of badge to be worn on a tunic. The centre panel was surrounded by tiny laurel leaves, exquisitely enamelled in dark green. The centre was a cartouche no more than three quarters of an inch wide. On it were the ornate letters CR. Turning it over, he saw more characters – RH 1643. He rubbed the reverse clean of dust and immediately believed it was gold. To say that Jamie was excited would be putting it mildly. He wrapped the small item back into the scrap of canvas and rushed out of the study in search of Paul Larkin. Eventually running him to earth in the stables, he grabbed unthinkingly at Larkin's sleeve.

"What on earth has got you in such a lather?" Larkin looked down at his young assistant who was almost incoherent with excitement.

"Master, I have found something amongst our discoveries that needs your immediate attention," he managed at last to make himself understood.

"Then, let us proceed quietly and calmly through the kitchen where we may collect ale, then go to the study where you may appraise me of this wondrous find."

Sat at either side of the small table, Jamie unwrapped the badge and passed it over to Larkin who looked at it, then picked it up for a closer inspection. Then he gave a low whistle.

"Now – first things first. Where and when was it found – the precise location and date, if you please."

Jamie referred to his notes. "It was found on the twenty-second day of August. I remember picking it up thinking it were no more than a discarded piece of canvas. It were in a shallow hole with one of the knives we found at the same time. It was at location one hundred and sixty-three – about a hundred yards west of the tiny hamlet of Scorriton – and that's south of Holne."

Jamie took the large map they had been producing and turned it so that Larkin could see it for himself.

"Aye – I remember that site," Larkin nodded. "An old man was walking his equally old dog along the track. I well remember him looking at us as if we were mad to be scrabbling about."

"Are the front initials what I think they are?" Jamie wondered.

"At a rough guess, I would say that they stand for Charles Rex – and that would be king Charles the first. 1643 was just about the time that he was appointing various new commanders. Prince Rupert had already proved himself to be totally inept. I wonder if RH refers to Lord Ralph Hopton?"

"Were he one of the new commanders?" Jamie asked.

"Aye – and one of the very few who knew what he was doing. He went into exile with Prince Charles – as he then was. I shall have to travel to Westminster to find out more. But first, I shall have a chat with Fisher. He, like I, ended up as a senior officer in Parliament's army and thus may know far more that do I."

Jamie looked so excited at the prospect that Kent took immediate pity on the young fellow.

"And as you discovered it and have kept such detailed notes, you shall accompany me."

Jamie rushed home that evening, full of his news. He found it hard to get to sleep that night. He had never travelled further than twenty miles from Bovey Tracey in his life.

Mary Cove was wife to Harry Cove, Bailiff. She was also the schoolmistress. In addition, she was mother to thirteen-year-old twins Will and Peterkin, plus mother to nine-year-old Lauren. She was not only a very intelligent woman, but as schoolmistress, highly preceptive. So, when she noted the twins whispering and giggling together for two days past, she immediately knew that the young lads were plotting something – and was determined to find out what it was.

"Harry, those twins are up to some devilment," she said that evening as the two sat before the fire.

"What? Again?" Harry grinned. "Last time it was salt in the ale. I administered dire punishment for that."

"Seven days helping to muck out pigs and byres," Mary nodded. "Seems they have yet to learn."

Lauren came in to say goodnight to her parents, who seized the opportunity to quiz their young daughter.

"Aye, mama – they are being very secret," Lauren confided. "They run into their bedroom and close the door on me. I have listened at the keyhole but cannot make out what it is they are whispering about."

"Have you not made out one single word?" Harry asked.

Lauren made her usual face when thinking deeply – brow furrowed, and mouth pursed.

"I *think* I heard them say the name Rachael, but I cannot be sure, papa."

Lauren demanded a goodnight kiss from mother and father, then skipped up the stairs to bed. Mary and Harry looked at one another.

"There is only one Rachael that I know of – Simon and Imelda's daughter," Harry grunted.

"And she is about the same age as the twins," Mary nodded. "Do you really believe those two are stupid enough to rouse Simon to anger? He would slaughter them if they did aught to his daughter."

"Perhaps what they are planning is not a prank but some sort of attempt to win that young maid's favour," Harry wondered. "After all, they are thirteen and Rachael is a very pretty girl!"

"But would they not be more likely to indulge in competition were such the case?"

"Upon second thoughts, that is probably not it," Harry again thought aloud. "Rachael is nearly a year older than the twins. She would not consider them as of interest. Nay – tis some devilment they are planning!"

"There is one person from whom no secret is safe – never has been," Mary had an idea. "Hob knows everybody and everything that is going on. I shall ask him to watch and learn. If anyone can discover what is afoot, Hob can!"

Mary went to find Hob and asked him to keep his eyes and ears open. May grinned at them both, knowing full well that Hob *would* find out. Her young husband was like a terrier after a rat when given such a mission.

It was the next day when Larkin, with Jamie as his close companion, met with Fisher. Larkin was anxious to learn as much as he could about Hopton. He was not so sure that either man would be able to further his knowledge about Templeton.

"Hopton?" Fisher raised a bushy eyebrow. "Right man in the wrong place at the wrong time! And serving the wrong master! Never stood a chance, well -not in my opinion. Why this sudden interest in him?"

Larkin took out the small badge that was wrapped in the old piece of canvas, unwrapped it and placed the precious object upon the table.

Fisher reached forward and placed the badge in the palm of his hand. He emitted a soft whistle.

"I now understand why this interest of yours," he grunted. "This is almost certainly a gift from the late Charles Stuart to Hopton. However, you shall never be able to return it to its original owner. Hopton fled with the younger Charles after Launceston. I have it on very good authority that he died in Bruges sometime in 1652 – so he did not last that long following his departure."

Fisher peered closely at the badge – his eyesight not as good as it once had been.

"Bloody good general wasted upon a fool's errand. But I'm sure that this king of ours would welcome it's return."

Larkin emitted a bark of laughter.

"And how, pray, may I accomplish that miraculous feat?" he snorted.

Fisher looked across at Larkin.

"You, my young friend, need to keep your ear closer to the ground. Charles and a goodly section of his court are due to arrive in Exeter in three days from now. They will obviously be housed in the bishop's palace – Rougemont is hardly suitable."

"No doubt with that wretched Villiers woman as his close companion!" Larkin scowled.

"But not his queen?" Jamie asked, somewhat naively.

"How that poor woman manages to retain her regal calm is beyond me," Fisher growled. "Not only does she have to witness her husband's blatant infidelities, she now has his eldest illegitimate son paraded under her nose!"

"James, Duke of Monmouth. Son of Lucy Walter and young Charles, when our latest king was barely out of children's clothing!" Larkin added.

"So, young Paul – get you to Exeter and seek audience. Wave that badge under enough important noses and you will almost certainly be granted a hearing."

"Bloody hell," Jamie whispered to himself, wondering whether he would be allowed to accompany his master.

Larkin then raised the other matter that concerned him. "I am sure that our esteemed Bailiff will also need to know more about the family called Templeton – as a very precious box found amongst the sack of items bears the name."

Fisher gave Jamie a broad smile.

"Perhaps you, young man, would scamper off and invite our reverend to join us. If anyone in this town could shed light on that family, it is he."

Jamie glanced at Larkin, received a nod, and scampered off as asked. Within a half hour, he was back with James Forbes in close attendance.

"Templeton?" the reverend asked, sinking gratefully into a chair. "I have some knowledge."

"I, personally, have none whatsoever," Larkin admitted. "Perhaps you would be so good as to relate all you know so that I can relay it to our bailiff."

Forbes regaled himself with a swallow of ale, cleared his throat and relaxed into the cushions.

"Angus Templeton," he began. "From his first name, you already have guessed at his origins – Scotland. The seventh Henry, that miserable man always peering into shadows, fearing treachery at every corner, sent his daughter Margaret to marry the then Scottish king. One of the Scottish escort was indeed this Angus. He accompanied Margaret into that wild country and was present at Edinburgh castle when she was accepted as their queen. However, he left behind in Westminster, his second son. William Templeton was at that time just twenty or so years of age. His mission was to follow on with the Templeton baggage train. He did not do so. Instead, rumour at the time had it that young William bribed his own escort to follow him down into the west country. Rumour also had it that he settled somewhere to the north of Dartmoor, purchasing a modest dwelling and reimbursing his conspirators with parts of the Templeton baggage. It is undoubtedly where this precious box comes from. Now, all this happened over one hundred and fifty years ago. Old Angus died shortly after returning to Scotland, his wife having predeceased him. The eldest son, I believe his name was Johnathan, died in some bloody skirmish soon thereafter. And that, gentlemen, is the sum of my knowledge."

"Well, it is far more than I had some moments ago," Larkin nodded. "Our bailiff will have to pursue his enquiries north of the moor. I wonder what he shall discover – or if there is anything at all to *be* discovered."

Larkin, on his return to Brimley, asked Jamie to make a fair copy of all that they had learned, then took himself off for a walk up towards the tavern where he intended to make a very late dinner.

Matthew Kent was making his way slowly back through the town when he happened to see coming up the street towards him, someone he had never noticed before – in the company of someone he knew very well. May was talking animatedly to her companion, a youngish woman who immediately struck Kent with her poise and beauty.

"I shall question May," he vowed to himself. "I would like to make this lady's acquaintance."

The opportunity presented itself the very next morning when May herself arrived at Brimley to see her good friend Meg.

"Pardon my asking," he began. "But who was the lady with you yesterday? I saw you walking together up the main street."

"Oh, that's easily explained," May replied. "She is my sister Maud. She does not venture out often as she has never properly recovered from the loss of our parents. She spins lace and makes the most intricate and wonderful designs. She lives where we all lived until mother and father died and I went to marry Hob."

"Er, would it at all possible for you to effect an introduction?" Kent was unusually tongue-tied.

May gave him a big grin. "Maud inherited all the beauty," she replied. "But I would certainly be more than willing to introduce you, as long as your intentions were honourable – which I am sure they most certainly are."

May could hardly contain her excitement as she went back home. Maud, at twenty-seven years of age, needed the attention of someone like Matthew Kent. She had been a voluntary recluse for far too long.

CHAPTER XI

It had been James Ramsey who had come up with the most plausible explanation as to why the king and his entourage had travelled to Exeter for Christmas.

"As I understand it," he said to the enlarged family gathering on the feast of Saint Stephen, "London is in such a state after that disastrous fire that, anyone who could escape the frantic work being carried out, would do so. And there is nobody better or morse suitably able to escape the mess than the king himself."

"And all he has to do is to impose himself upon some poor devil," Avril laughed. "The bishop will be impoverished for years to come!"

Consequently, Paul Larkin and Jamie Ramsey set out on the ride to Exeter on the twenty-seventh day od December. Both were dressed in their finest apparel under the warmest cloaks they could find. Larkin had the badge wrapped in its canvas secreted in his innermost pocket. The ride in freezing cold weather took them just under three hours. They found themselves halted at the imposing gates of the bishop's palace.

Armed sentries – and there seemed to be many of them – demanded to know their business.

"I have in my possession an item that will be of great interest to the king. I shall deliver it only into his hands," Larkin stated.

"And I have the crown jewels tucked away in my breeches," the sergeant of the guard replied with a grin. "You'll have to do better than that to be admitted!"

"In that case, I shall show you the item in question and explain its importance. Please rest assured that I am not reaching for a pistol. I am not such an idiot to draw upon ten armed guards."

"Believe me, I have seen every shade of idiot – tall, short, fat, thin, from the barely literate right up to the well-spoken – such as yourself!"

Larkin produced the small piece of canvas and unwrapped it, then held it up well out of reach of the sergeant.

"Looks a pretty thing," the man admitted. "Why is it of interest to His Majesty?"

"It bears the inscription of his own father, a present to Sir Ralph Hopton."

That stopped the sergeant for a moment. "And how may I know that it's genuine?" he enquired.

"That I do not even know myself. Only His Majesty can judge that. And that is why I must deliver it personally to ask for his judgement."

"Then you must stay right there whilst I send for an authority." The sergeant beckoned one of his soldiers to go and fetch a member of the king's entourage.

It was a full half hour later when the sentry reappeared alongside a large and very important looking individual. Larkin was not in the least surprised to see this individual.

"Good day, my lord," he bowed his head.

Edward Hyde – Lord Clarendon – searched his memory. "Larkin, is it not?" he said.

"Yes, my lord. Paul Larkin. I was a colonel in service to parliament in its latter days."

"And you say you have a badge presented to Lord Hopton."

"Aye, my lord. I have. My young companion and I have been undertaking a detailed study of Dartmoor and simply came across it wrapped in this old piece of canvas."

Larkin unwrapped the badge and put it into the large and pudgy hand of the king's chief advisor. Clarendon's eyebrows rose several notches. He simply handed it back.

"Then you and this young fellow had better come with me. You may leave your horses with the sentries. They will be fed and cared for."

Larkin and Jamie dismounted and walked a pace behind Clarendon, through a massive pair of oaken doors, along a corridor and into a large hall where an imposing chair was stationed at the far end. In it sat King Charles II; on a stool by his side was an imposing woman – but certainly to Larkin's knowledge – not the queen. He (rightly) supposed it to be Barbara Villiers – the king's long-time mistress by whom he had fathered five children at the latest count.

Jamie was quite overawed to be in the presence of the king, but not exactly filled with awe at the spectacle of the figure that sprawled in that huge chair. A thin mouth was surmounted by an equally thin moustache. A massive wig of deep, brown hair curled down past shoulders that were supporting a full coat of silk. The legs, encased in white silk stopped at shoes of deepest black with tall heels.

"Majesty," Clarendon bowed. "Master Larkin and his servant have brought a relic of your own royal father."

Charles said nothing – reached out a hand to receive the badge, gave it a passing glance, and handed it to his chief advisor.

"I have one similar," he said, almost as if he was bored with the matter. "Hopton – and this is certainly his – had one, as did Rupert and Wentworth amongst many others. See that it is kept safe among my belongings. These two have been of service to us. See that they are properly rewarded."

The king waved a desultory hand in dismissal. Larkin, knowing the form, bowed and took three backward steps before turning to march out. Jamie, still in a sort of daze, followed him.

Clarendon followed them out of the hall, then halted as the doors were closed behind them. He seemed almost apologetic. He led them to a smaller room where a host of clerks were busy scribbling. He went to one particular desk and lifted a heavy purse which he handed silently to Paul Larkin.

"With His Majesty's best wishes and thanks," he said. Again, Larkin bowed before being led by a servant back the way the had come. Mounted once again, the rode off in silence.

"And what did you make of all that?" he grinned at Jamie once they were well out of earshot.

"Pompous fart!" Jamie retorted. "And I don't care if that's an act of treason!"

"And did you note the lady at his side?"

"Yes – was that the queen?"

"No – that was Barbara Villiers
, mother of at least five of his bastards. God alone knows how many there really are scattered over Europe."

"And that is who all the fuss has been about? If I'd known, I would have wanted parliament to stay in power. He's hardly impressive, is he?"

"No – impressive he most certainly is not. But we have done our duty. So let us find a tavern and have a splendid dinner and divide the spoils."

Jamie rode back home at Larkin's side, his own purse being heavier by ten gold coins. It was more than he would have earned in five years.

May was as good as her word. She had thought long and hard about a seemingly innocent way that her sister and Matthew Kent might be in the same place at the same time. She was very pleased with the outcome of her planning. What, she asked herself, could possibly go wrong?

She had deliberately not consulted her husband as she knew full well that Hob's plans had at times yielded exactly the opposite of those that had been intended – or so they had when he had been a young terror.

What was needed, she reasoned, was the calm and uncomplicated planning of a female mind – no unnecessary subterfuge that could so easily yield the opposite of the desired result. Consequently, she planned a quiet and uncomplicated way in which the meeting could be arranged. Maud, she knew, would shy away from anything she did not understand.

That in itself was not easy. She, Hob and their daughters lived in the same large house as Harry, Mary, the twins and their younger sister. Only Mary was allowed into her confidence.

"Matthew is interested in meeting Maud?" Mary's reaction was thrilled. "It is just what the dear soul needs. Now, how do you plan to achieve this?"

When May outlined her plan, Mary was impressed with its simplicity. "We shall all be very happy to attend – and to act as if nothing was afoot.

She first made sure that her 'guest' was able to attend the meeting, then visited the cottage at Brimley to tell Kent of the plan – and to warn him to act as if nothing untoward was happening.

On the last day of December, Maud turned up at Parke with some samples of her lace work. May had made absolutely sure that Hob, their children, Harry and the twins and their sister were all absent for the morning. Only Mary was there when the 'guest' arrived – an old established haberdasher from Ashburton. Phase one accomplished – Maud was at the house.

One hour later, the haberdasher left having given Maud an order for lace trimmings for cuffs – the latest fashion. Maud was delighted with the result and was being congratulated when there came a knock at the door.

Matthew Kent had arrived just as the haberdasher was leaving – no coincidence as Kent had been lurking in the lane waiting for that to happen.

As Mary answered the knock, Matthew put on his best bland face and asked if the bailiff was in.

"No, not until later this afternoon," Mary answered, deadpan. "But – please come in and join us in a glass of mead to celebrate."

Matthew came into the large parlour and greeted May, then looked questioningly at Maud.

"Oh, Master Kent – pray let me introduce my sister Maud. Maud, my dear, this is Master Kent."

Kent extended a hand and bent slightly over the proffered fingers. "I understand that there is something to celebrate," he said.

"Indeed, there most certainly is," May answered. "Maud has just received a commission for lace trimmings – a substantial commission!"

"Then I shall be very happy to raise my glass to congratulate you," Kent managed not to look too closely into a pair of startlingly blue eyes. Maud was indeed a beautiful woman, he thought.

After a good half-hour, Kent realised that he was probably overstaying his welcome. As he made to rise from his chair, Mary then put the finishing touches to the plan.

"Matthew – are you on your way to the tavern by any chance?"

"As it happens, I am indeed," Kent nodded.

"Then may we entrust Maud to your care as her home is on your way?"

And so the plan, as far as it went, had worked. Kent offered his arm and escorted Maud to the gates of Parke. The rest was now up to him.

"I have had a thought," he said as they approached the crossroads. "I am holding a small gathering at Brimley this evening – to see in the new year. Colonel Larkin has agreed to it, but cannot be there himself. Mary and your sister will be there as well as their husbands and children. I would be delighted to welcome you also – it would be a further opportunity to celebrate your excellent fortune."

Maud was not in the slightest bit deceived by all these goings-on. "May, you conniving vixen," she thought.

But for some reason, she accepted the invitation and would travel with her sister and family. For the first time in many a long day, she was rather taken with this perfectly mannered man. He was well liked and trusted by everyone – although she had never met him before that day. She was human enough to wonder where that all might lead.

CHAPTER XII

Many 'gatherings' were held in Bovey Tracey that evening. Most people seemed quietly confident that the new year of 1667 would see a general improvement. But not all. Some viewed another year with resignation. Two such were sitting together around the blazing fire at the rectory.

The Reverend James Forbes, and his equally aged friend Fisher, gazed at the orange flames that surmounted the pile of logs that were radiating a comforting heat. They were, as usual, reminiscing.

"What do you remember of the plague of 1603?" Forbes asked after a period of silent introspection.

"Little, thank the Good Lord," Fisher answered with a grunt. "I was just three years old and remember nothing of the time itself. All I remember is the story told to me repeatedly by my dear mother."

"I was of similar age," Forbes nodded. "But – one thing hangs in my memory. It was the same year that James became king of England as well as of Scotland. Many people at the time said that the visitation of plague was the result of such union – and that it would reappear every time another Stuart occupied this throne."

"Didn't happen when Charles became king in 1625!" Fisher muttered.

"No, plague did not reappear. But other dreadful things had their beginnings!"

Fisher was somewhat astonished to hear his old friend talk in such a manner.

"I always believed you to be a staunch believer in the rightness of all that he did," he charged his friend.

"Upon very sober reflection on what it all led to, I have had to revise some of my former beliefs," Forbes admitted. "I see now that his intransigence was misplaced. He should have engaged in serious dialogue instead of turning a haughty shoulder on his detractors."

"And what of his son – the one to whom you were chaplain for some years?"

"This is for your ears only, my old friend. I am at the point of despair whenever I contemplate the debauchery of the present court. It is as if license has been granted for any behaviour. Apart from his championing the arts and sciences, I see no good whatsoever in this new king of ours!"

And that, Fisher thought, was a startling revelation from his comrade – but one with which he was in total agreement.

Brimley was ablaze with light – candles and lanterns casting a warm and happy glow from all the downstairs windows. Maud had travelled with her sister and May's family, and all had been warmly welcomed. She was happily surprised to see that Luke Farmer, the steward, plus all the staff had been invited to celebrate the coming year.

Hob found an ideal opportunity to gather Harry and Mary into a quiet corner. He had much to tell them.

"Concerning the twin's prank," he began quietly. "I made a start, not with the twins, but with the supposed recipient of the prank – Rachael. It seems that young Rachel has received a letter of a somewhat amorous nature from Billy Longtree, the son of farmer Longtree down on the heath. She is perplexed to say the least as she never expected to receive such a missive from that source!"

Mary pounced immediately on the obvious flaw.

"Billy, to my certain knowledge, can neither read nor write," she said. "He was not blessed with normal wits. He is, to use the accepted phrase, simple-minded. He is a happy lad, always laughing at what one would expect to find amusing to a child of five. He most definitely would never have communicated any feelings of an amorous nature to Rachael. Are you implying that the twins are responsible?"

"It seems the most likely explanation," Hob nodded.

"Then, believe me, I shall know for certain if I can have sight of the letter," Mary replied.

"Has Rachael shown the letter to his father?" Harry asked a rather important question.

"I doubt it," Hob almost grinned. "Simon would have made a beeline for Billy had he been aware of it."

"Then you and I, Mary, shall have to see Rachael first thing in the morning. We have to stop this immediately – or our twins might find themselves in very deep water."

"If, indeed, they are responsible," Mary cautioned.

Kent, as host, had to make sure that he divided his time equitably between all his guests. That gave him a slight problem – how to speak on a one-to-one basis with Maud. He had worked out that Maud was two years younger than her sister May, and that made Maud about twenty-seven years old. Most girls were married at seventeen or eighteen. Some, like Ella, had been married even earlier. Something had obviously held the rather lovely Maud back from seeking marriage. May had given him some insight into the reason, but Kent was sure there was a deeper reason somewhere. But how to go about discovering it?

Kent himself was eight years older than Maud. At thirty-five, Kent was not that unusual in marrying late. Many men of business did. His earlier life had been devoted to roving the countryside upon some mission or other for parliament.

Then, somewhere approaching ten o'clock, the opportunity arose. Maud was on her own looking at the portrait of Lady Violette that hung at one corner of the great hall. Matthew wandered across.

May, ever vigilant, saw what was happening and placed herself strategically to intercept and waylay anyone wandering in that direction.

"She was a remarkable old lady," Kent said as he came up behind Maud.

"Indeed, she was," Maud agreed. A small part of her was amused to see how Matthew managed this next bit. The main part of her remained on guard!

Kent knew that he could well blow his chances out of the water if he did not act decisively, using oblique language instead of direct speech.

"Your sister tells me that you lead a somewhat reclusive life," he began, looking directly into those startlingly blue eyes. "I would dearly like to know you better, if only you would afford me the chance." There – the die was cast.

Maud coloured slightly. "It is perfectly true that I have shut myself away – ever since our mother and father were so cruelly taken by the winter fever. I found that it helped me to cope better with the loss – until it became a habit. But I am still happy in my own company."

"And not the merest chink of light for someone who would dearly like to know you better?"

Maud, despite all her ingrained defensiveness, felt some real rapport with this man. Perhaps it was indeed time for her to admit someone other than her sister and nieces into her world.

"And how would you propose setting about that task?" she said very quietly.

"First, by inviting you to take dinner with me, chaperoned, if that would make you more comfortable."

"Master Kent – do you not feel that we are past the age to need chaperones? I feel that I could trust you to remain a perfect gentleman."

"Does that answer imply acceptance of my invitation?"

"Yes, Master Kent. I should be very pleased to accept your kind invitation."

"Then let us forego the Master Kent, shall we? My name is Matthew."

"And mine is Maud, as you are fully aware."

"Then I shall make sure that the dinner is of the very best quality. Shall we say this coming Saturday?"

"That would be very acceptable - and thank you. Perhaps now, we can relieve my poor sister from her sentry duty!"

Kent, who had not been aware of May's strategy, looked around and burst out laughing.

The next morning, the first day of the new year, saw Harry and Mary at the door of the smithy – closed as it was deemed a holiday. Imelda answered the knock and gave her visitors a big grin of welcome.

"May we have a word with Rachael?" Mary asked.

Imelda immediately thought that this had something to do with Mary's position as schoolmistress – and saw nothing at all strange in the request. She called for her daughter to come and join the two visitors in the parlour.

As Rachael arrived, Imelda closed the door behind her as she left.

"I shall give you privacy – it is obviously something to do with schoolwork," she said.

Rachael, a rather pretty girl of fourteen, sat down, hands clasped in her lap. Not for one second did she anticipate the way this interview was about to go.

Harry was content to let Mary lead the next part.

"Rachael," Mary began quietly. "Please do not be upset, but have you recently received a rather disturbing letter supposedly sent to you by Billy?"

Rachael seemed on the point of tears as she nodded. "I could scarcely believe it when I read it," she said. "I never for a moment thought that Billy could do such a thing."

"Billy almost certainly did not," Mary put a comforting arm about Rachael's shoulders. "Do you still have this letter?"

In answer, Rachael produced a large piece of paper from the pocket of her pinafore. Silently, she handed it to Mary. Harry moved behind his wife so that both could read it.

'Dear Rachael,' the letter commenced in somewhat spidery writing – written in a vivid violet ink. 'I have long admired you from afar, the way you walk and the manner in which you smile with those perfect lips. How much would I long to kiss them! Please allow me to tell you in person how much I desire to be near you, to hold you tight to me. Yours in utter devotion," it was signed Billy Longtrees – in even more spidery writing.

"Rachael, look at me please," Mary turned the young face to hers. "This did *not* come from Billy. He, to my certain knowledge, cannot write to save his life. This is a hoax – and I am afraid that both Harry and I know only too well from whom it *did* come."

"Unfortunately, we do," Harry agreed. He was seething angry at his twin sons. This was not a mere prank – it was cruel. "I am going to ask your parents to come and witness what we propose to do about it. No blame whatsoever can be attached to you, and both Mary and I will make sure that they know this."

Harry went to the door and went in search of Simon and Imelda. The two read the letter silently. Simon was on the point of a massive eruption when he handed it back.

"I'll skin the little sod!" he growled, making ready to set about that task.

"Simon – Billy never wrote this. He, in all probability, knows nothing whatsoever about it. Both Mary and I know who did, and I would ask that you let us deal with it in our own way. At this precise moment, I ask you simply to believe that you will witness an abject apology given to Rachael, and another to poor Billy."

Rachael, slightly quicker on the uptake, gave a gasp.

"Are you saying that Will and Peterkin sent this?" she asked.

"Almost certainly they did," Harry said. "And they shall pay a very heavy price for it. Not only have they betrayed you, they have shamed poor Billy. That colour of ink comes from my own desk. Mary and I are mortified that our own children have caused such distress. They will shortly live to regret it!"

"Speaking for myself, I would never have thought those two capable of it," Imelda had a soft spot for the twins.

"Much as it goes against my inclination, I trust both of you to deal with this. However, please let them know that, should they ever attempt to hurt my little girl again, I shall flay the skin from their backs!" Simon said between clenched teeth.

"Oh, believe me, when we have finished with them, they will be heartily sick and tired of the sight of the place they shall be working. Mary and I shall bring them here this very afternoon to beg forgiveness."

Harry and Mary walked back home in silence. Both were shamed by the actions of their twins and were adamant in their determination to wreak havoc on their young lives.

The twins were summoned by a roar from their father the moment that they entered the house. Two thirteen-year-old boys stood side by side in the large parlour.

"You two have brought utter shame upon us and upon yourselves," Harry shouted, caring not a whit who heard. "You wrote an appalling letter to Rachael. You have hurt and shamed her. You made it seem to come from young Billy. You have shamed him also. Why? And do not dare compound your guilt by lying!"

"But, papa, it was merely a jest," Will ventured.

"A jest? A jest, you say. Hear that Mary – our sons believe it to have been merely a jest!"

"It was a wicked deception – and one that you are going to bitterly regret!" Mary could barely look at them.

"You will now go to your room and remain there until we call you down after dinner – a dinner in which you will not participate. Then you shall accompany us to the smithy where you will beg forgiveness from Rachael. She is bitterly upset by your wicked letter. Thank your lucky stars that Simon has agreed to leave this in our hands. What he would do to you otherwise I leave to your imagination. And then you will come with us to ask pardon from Billy."

Peterkin managed a look of hope that this would be an end to the matter. Harry knew that look.

"And then you will commence your real punishment. You will attend the pigsty every day from dawn to dusk. You will muck out, feed, and clean the pigs. You will speak to nobody but one another. You will take your meals, such as they will be, at the pigsty. At dusk, you will bathe and stay in your rooms until dawn the next day. You have one month to learn the error of your ways."

"And do not look to your sister for help and succour," Mary added. "When she learns of your disgraceful conduct, she will be as angry as we are!"

"But mama – it really *was* simply a harmless jest," Will tried again.

"Harmless? No, Will. It was not harmless. It was hurtful, spiteful, and cruel. I am ashamed of you!"

And that, from their mother, brought it home more than anything else would have. They idolised their mother.

CHAPTER XIII

Because Harry, Mary and family lived in the same large house as Hob, May and their two daughters, it was imperative that everyone knew why the twins were to spend their days with the pigs. It was therefore also necessary that Luke Barton, Grace, plus all other members of the staff were also informed. The twins were shunned as a consequence.

Will, being ever hopeful, made one attempt to enlist the help of his sister. Lauren, utterly disgusted with what they had done, reported immediately to Harry – who reduced their rations as a result.

January of 1667 ground on with intermittent snow, biting winds, occasional sunshine, and bouts of sleet. However, much to the huge relief of Avril and James, no sign of another outbreak of the winter fever. For such small mercies, may we be truly thankful, Avril muttered as each day passed without a call from some stricken individual.

On the last Friday of January, Harry received a visitor – a tall and imposing individual who introduced himself as Leonard Greatorex, a Crown Agent. He had arrived alone, riding a very impressive black horse, leather and brass-work glinting in the watery sunshine. Seated in Harry's office, this individual came straight to the point of his visit.

"I have been sent here to take possession of the items that were found on Parke land," he announced in a voice that had the timbre of authority.

"The candlesticks have already been returned to their rightful owner," Harry interrupted.

"Then, they should not have been. I require you to repossess them."

On the pretext of going to fetch the remaining items, Harry left Greatorex in his office and went in search of Hob. To nobody's surprise, Hob was in the kitchen 'testing' the latest batch of sweet pastries.

"Hob," Harry said very quietly. "Go immediately to the cottage and fetch Master Kent here. I have someone with me who *says* he is a Crown Agent. If anyone can test the veracity of that, it is Matthew."

Harry then took his time retrieving the items from the strong box in the cellar, finally returning to his office. He arranged the ornate dagger, the beautiful box, and the large purse of coins on his table. He could hardly have failed to notice that the eyes of his visitor were locked firmly upon that bulging purse.

Harry craftily shifted the purse to his side of the large desk and put the box firmly in the centre.

"Inside is a name Angus Templeton," he said. "Have you any news of who is the current owner?"

"Ah, yes – Templeton. Originally part of the escort for Margaret Tudor when she travelled to Scotland to marry their king James IV. Never returned. His younger brother, Alexander, remained in the Templeton home not that far distant in Dorset. I would imagine that ownership rests with whoever now holds title to the small manor."

"And your brief is what exactly?"

"Simple and straightforward – to take possession of *all* the items and to have them properly assessed by the exchequer."

"Then, a part of your mission is part accomplished already," Harry could not supress a small smile. "The candlesticks are already in Westminster – or wherever Queen Catherine resides. They were a present to Her Majesty from Lady Groombridge – who was furious when they disappeared, but delighted when they were returned."

Greatorex was about to make a rejoinder when there came a tap at the door. It opened to reveal his friend Matthew Kent.

"Ah, Matthew – this is indeed a happy coincidence. Please meet Leonard Greatorex, a Crown Agent. Master Greatorex – Matthew Kent, one-time parliamentary agent."

"Then, as a Crown Agent, you will be well acquainted with Lord Ashley – or Lord Shaftesbury as he now is. Harry, Lord Ashley is Chancellor of the exchequer – to whom all financial agents report."

"Of course – I report to him on a weekly basis," came the firm reply.

"And you will naturally carry his seal of authority," Kent prompted.

Greatorex drew himself up haughtily.

"Are you, sir, questioning my bona fides?"

"No, sir – simply establishing them," Kent replied.

Greatorex reached inside his embroidered tunic and placed an elaborate seal attached to a parchment. Kent saw immediately that it was a genuine seal. However, the warrant to which it was attached was 'open' – in that the holder was not specified by name. He said nothing but gave a polite nod. The warrant was folded and placed inside the tunic.

Harry gave Kent an enquiring glance, receiving a bland expression in return.

"As already stated, the six candlesticks are no longer here and cannot be reached," he restarted the original conversation. "You have given me the necessary information concerning the box. Ownership of the dagger is unknown – and ownership of the coins can never be proved. It is my duty to contact a surviving Templeton and ascertain how and when this elaborate box was missed."

"My warrant – which this gentleman has seen – is the only authority you need obey," Greatorex retorted angrily.

"Your warrant, sir, states that every help and assistance must be afforded the holder in pursuance of his duties!" Kent interrupted.

"Precisely!"

"It does not state, however, the nature of those duties."

"If you have ever had dealings with parliament, you will know that specific duties and missions are seldom specified in precise detail. It is often thought prudent to offer the holder the widest scope in his endeavours!"

"Precisely so," Kent agreed. "But to my certain knowledge, the person to whom the warrant is granted is invariably named within the text. The warrant you showed makes no mention of the identity of the holder!"

Greatorex stood up and faced Kent square-on. Harry immediately stood up on his side of the desk.

"Do you dare accuse me of deception?" Greatorex almost shouted in Kent's face.

"No sir, I merely point to a glaring anomaly that *might* give rise to suspicion," Kent replied as quietly as Greatorex's explosion had been loud.

Harry believed that the ball was firmly in his court. He gave a loud snort and resumed his seat when he saw that Greatorex was noise over substance.

"My obvious next move is to travel to Exeter to seek the advice of the sheriff," he announced, gathering all the items to his side of the desk. "If, having examined the evidence the sheriff decides that the items be placed into your care, then I shall do so. If not, then I most assuredly shall not."

"For a minor, county functionary, you take upon yourself the risk of incurring the great displeasure of people close to the king himself. You will regret this – and I shall make it my mission to see that you pay a heavy price!" Greatorex attempted browbeating.

"I wonder," Harry sat and twiddled his thumbs. "Our rector, James Forbes, was personal chaplain to His Majesty when he was the young Prince of Wales. I have little doubt that the reverend could be prevailed upon to intercede in this matter – relying upon that former relationship."

"That is a good thought," Kent agreed. "Perhaps, Master Greatorex, you would be willing to hold this matter in abeyance until such enquiries bear fruit?"

"I shall write a letter of explanation for Reverend Forbes to forward to His Majesty," Harry warmed to the theme.

"I warn you both that you are embarking upon a hazardous path," Greatorex shouted. "To thwart the orders of the Chancellor is to court personal disaster. Once again, I *demand* that you do as I am authorised to order – hand over those items immediately!"

"The warrant you showed me bore the seal of Lord Ashley – and he is *not* the Chancellor. Lord Clarendon holds that post," Kent pointed out.

Greatorex went to the door, paused and faced the two men. "I shall also travel to Exeter," he stormed. "I shall show my warrant to the sheriff and demand your immediate arrest, plus seizure of those items."

He stomped out of the office, leaving the door wide open. Unsurprisingly, a curly head appeared in place of the angry man. Hob was never far distant when any sort of trouble threatened.

"Heard all that," he said. "Want me to see where he goes?"

Harry grinned and nodded. "Come back when you deem it safe to do so," he said. He turned to Kent. "You believe this man to be an impersonator?" he queried.

"Too many inconsistencies," Kent replied quietly. "Bluster, wrong names, absence of detail – of course, he just *may* be genuine. In which case, we have some explaining to do. But I do not think so."

Hob reappeared about an hour later, munching on a sweet pastry. With Hob, food always took preference. He slumped into a chair and grinned.

"Loudmouth is in the tavern partaking of a hearty dinner, plus when I left, his third large mug of Sal's lethal brew."

Harry got up and went in search of Sam Garvey and Robert Hook. These two, expert trackers in the past, were ideal for his purpose.

"In the tavern is a certain Master Greatorex," he told them. "Sooner or later, he will leave on horseback. I need you to follow him and let me know where he goes, whom he sees – if anyone – and where he ends up."

"And he is not to know of our presence?" Garvey queried.

"Absolutely not!"

"Then, master bailiff, he shall not be aware of us," Garvey grinned.

Reverend James Forbes sat and read the long letter aloud to his old friend Fisher. Harry sat patiently as Forbes came to the end.

"Very succinct, if I may say so," Forbes glanced over at Harry. "And you wish me to append my signature to it and have it delivered to His Majesty?"

"That's the plan," Harry nodded.

"Then, I shall have to make a very few amendments. You are relying upon a very distant relationship – one the king may well have difficulty calling to mind. Also, there is the problem of it actually reaching the king. There will be numerous stages that it will have to pass through – and any one of them may not forward it to the next."

"Aye, reverend – I am fully aware of that," Harry agreed. "But the most important thing is that it is *seen* and *known* to have been written and sent."

"And you have those bloodhounds following this chap?" Forbes asked.

"They used to be the very best. I wonder where this man will actually go. His obvious route will take him to Exeter and the sheriff. Matthew Kent is almost convinced he will go nowhere near the place."

"Then, I shall make the necessary amendments to this letter and send it on its way. But do not be surprised if that is the last anyone ever sees of it," Forbes said with a smile.

Kent, meanwhile, was entertaining a rather curious Maud to an afternoon at the fireside in his cottage. He had ordered a sweet cordial and small cakes to be served. Maud was quite intrigued. Was this somewhat rich man paying her court? Why would he, a landowner of wealth, seek the company of a lacemaker whose father had been hedger and ditcher?

Being like her sister May, a woman of direct speech, she broke into a period of silence with exactly that question.

"Master Kent, whilst I am flattered that you would seek my company, it is surely apparent that I am not of your class and station. I am intrigued why you would seek me out when there must be ladies of more suitable station eager to make your acquaintance."

Kent knew that he had to answer just as directly. "I agree that there are ladies of my social standing who might well be agreeable to meet me. But I am not, and never have been, conscious of social station – as you put it. My past is an open book. For many years I was a simple employee of parliament, going hither and yon on missions that even now I am unable to relate. I was a functionary, an employee. I saved diligently during this period. But it was not until I received a wholly unexpected bequest that I was able to purchase this house. Please note the use of 'purchase'. I did not inherit, I purchased. Had I made your acquaintance when a mere employee, nobody would have raised an eyebrow. But I am still that same person – I like to think that I have not changed. Agreed, my social standing has changed in that I am a small landowner. But I have not. So, why you, you ask. Let me be totally frank and open with you – as you rightly deserve. The work that you produce is exquisite. It marks you as a person of refinement and excellent taste. Were you not, you would have had to copy the work of others. On a far more personal level, I see in you a lady of great beauty, a lady I would wish to know far better. I also would have you believe that I have no base motive; I simply want to have your company so that we may – hopefully – develop a relationship that is as close as possible."

Maud listened to this in silence. Was this actually a suggestion of the beginnings of a courtship?

"That sounds as if you wish to pay me court, Master Kent."

"Yes, it does, does it not," Kent smiled. "Would it be so strange if that were the case? And pray drop the Master Kent. My name is Matthew."

"Then, Matthew, to me it is strange indeed. I have shunned relationships as you are no doubt aware from my sister – who I know for certain you have approached."

"Is it so strange that you would never countenance it?"

"Actually, no, it would not," Maud replied honestly.

"Then that, at least, gives me some hope. You deserve nothing but honesty, and that is what I shall give you. It is my earnest desire to pay court to you in the fond hope that, in the fullness of time, you will reciprocate those feelings and accept a proposal of marriage."

Maud had felt all along that this was where it was leading. Did she want such an outcome? And if not, why not? Could she actually see herself as eventual Mistress Kent?

"You have given me much food for thought," she said after a long pause. "Would you believe it unreasonable that I take time to process it all?"

"I would be surprised if you did not," Kent nodded. "Please, take all the time you require; consult whomsoever you wish. My feelings will not change, I assure you."

"Then I shall give you my answer in two days from now –
when I attend the dinner you promised me."

And with that, Kent had to be satisfied.

It was past dinner the next day when Sam Garvey knocked at
the bailiff's door. He was spattered in mud and very cold. Harry
sat him by the fire to thaw out.

"Went nowhere near Exeter, Master Bailiff," he began when
his teeth had stopped chattering. "And, before you ask, he was
never once aware of two ferrets following him. No, not Exeter as
I said. He rode south once he had reached Chudleigh Knighton.
I suppose he started out that way in case anyone remarked on him
going towards Exeter. But he then went south and rode until
sunset to Littlehempston, where he spent the night in the tavern.
Haddock and I had to make do with a dilapidated barn! Then, this
very morning, off he went again, this time westward to the
village of Staverton. Just by the bridge over the Dart stands a
large house. He stopped there and had his horse stabled by an
ostler. He went into that house exactly like an owner would. We
then turned tail and reported back as soon as we could."

"Then, you have done really excellent work – for which I
thank you. It will certainly be reflected in your pay."

So, mused Harry when Garvey had gone to get warm and
changed. Staverton, is it? Kent was absolutely right. I must get
that information to him right now.

CHAPTER XIV

On the second day of February, under lowering skies that threatened rain at any moment, Nell and Kate arrived at the smallholding. The next day would be Jamie's eighteenth birthday.

Kate was immediately whisked off by Rosie to go and see the chickens – many of whom had small, fluffy chicks with them. Gil and Ella, only too glad for a break in the never-ending work of the smallholding, settled down in the parlour with Nell.

"Cannot Adam take the time off from the business?" Gil enquired.

"Unfortunately, he cannot. But it is not *our* business that keeps him away," Nell replied, a worried look on her face. "No – tis his father's business that keeps him occupied and deeply concerned."

"I trust his father is not ailing," Ella was always worried about the winter fever.

"No, hardly ailing in body," Nell replied. "Word came to Adam not a week past that his father has been persuaded to take a part share in a new trading venture. Two wealthy merchants from Bristol have managed to cajole him into joining with them to participate in this filthy slaving business."

"That is appalling news," Gil was horrified. He had met Clements senior on a few occasions and had been impressed by the man's sense of what was right and proper.

"As soon as Adam had learned of it, he told me immediately. I agreed that he must go straight away and endeavour to put a stop to it. To be associated, however distantly, with this vile business is not to be borne!"

"And what hope do you suppose Adam has of persuading his father?" Ella asked.

"In all honesty, little or none," Nell answered, close to tears. "His father has always been single-minded – once an idea takes root, none but an archangel can shake him from it!"

"But who, with you here and Adam with his father, is minding *your* business?" Gil wanted to know.

"Oh, we have now an excellent manager down at the dockside. He will take good care for the few days I am here."

"But, now to happier matters," Ella was determined to make her young friend's stay a happy one. "Jamie is totally immersed in the business up on the moor. He has spent all winter making notes on the findings – and the conclusions drawn from them. Believe it or not, he has not even spared a glance at any of the girls in the town. He is slowly becoming a reclusive monk, content with his studies."

"And I understand that Rosie also eschews male company," Nell grinned, her mood lightening by the minute.

"No, I think she does not eschew male company. I do believe she is hardly aware of them at all! Like her brother, she immerses herself in herbs, medicines, study of illness and the reasons for it."

"That must not be easy for you with no sign of grandchildren forthcoming."

"Oh, there is as yet no reason for worry. Neither is yet beyond all hope," Ella laughed.

Nell regarded her friend with a wry smile.

"I sense some subterfuge behind that remark," she prompted.

"I am fairly certain that young Hal Farmer is more than simply interested in our Rosie," Ella admitted.

"What? Hal from Brimley? The son of Luke and Meg? Why was I not aware of this?" Gil demanded.

"That, my esteemed husband, is because you are not a woman," Ella gave Gil a sweet smile. "It does not take a genius to work it out – not when the young man in question hovers about looking like a lovesick puppy."

"Well, I suppose they are of an age," Gil admitted. "He is well out of his juvenile pranks, rather like Jack Smith."

"And who is minding your home whilst you and Adam are away?" Ella changed the subject.

"Oh, Lottie is growing into the role very well. She already is companion and nursemaid to Kate – and will make an excellent housekeeper in time."

"Then all we now need is for Adam to succeed with his father," Ella was determined to turn the conversation to happier matters.

"It is but a fond hope," Nell answered. "Adam will be mortified if his father continues along that path. He is of like mind with me on the subject – that the so-called trade is evil, heartless, and brings shame upon any who participate in it."

Maud Fletcher grabbed the first opportunity to go and confer with her sister. She had contemplated going to see Mary but on second thoughts, decided to keep it 'in the family'. Consequently, she grabbed the next dry and relatively warm day to walk to Parke, knowing that Hob would be about his work for Harry and that young Kitty and Poppy would be at school. She found her sister in the kitchen conferring with cook. May caught the beckoning glance and took Maud to her bedroom.

"Don't tell me," May grinned. "Let me guess – Master Matthew Kent!"

"Am I really that transparent?" Maud replied with a rueful smile. "But yes, it is all about that gentleman. He completely unburdened himself to me and made no subterfuge at all. His intention is to pay court to me with a view to an eventual proposal of marriage. On a point of honesty, I cannot fault him."

"So, score one hit to Master Kent," May poked one finger in the air. "Believe me, honesty in a relationship is a priceless asset. But let us get down to the basic issue. First, do you want to be married? Not necessarily to Matthew, but married at all?"

Unhesitatingly, Maud nodded. "Yes, I do."

"So, first hurdle overcome. Next – do you like Matthew?"

Again, a very affirmative nod.

"Third question – do you trust him in all things?"

"Based upon our limited acquaintance, yes."

"Question four – do you believe that he respects you?"

"Again, so far, yes, I do."

"And do you see in him a person with whom you could envisage spending your life?"

"Yes, I suppose I do."

"Then, dearest little sister, what in the name of heaven are you consulting me for? It seems to me that you have the answers you require. Marriage, like any commitment, is always a gamble. You weigh up the points for and the points against. You seem already to have done precisely that. My advice, follow your own good instincts."

"I am dining with him tomorrow. At the end of the evening, I shall give him my answer – that I am willing for him to pay court as he wishes."

"Let him court you for as long as you need to know him inside and out. He is a sensitive man and will know when the time is right to voice his proposal."

"You like him, do you not?"

"I do not know anyone hereabouts who does not!"

May took her sister down for a glass of cordial and a griddle cake. Maud reflected as she drank and ate. She knew that would have been the exact result had she confided in Mary. She also wondered why she had made the trip at all – she had merely received confirmation of her own thoughts!

Matthew Kent missed seeing Mad by two hours; he arrived at Parke after dinner with his latest thoughts about the man Greatorex. Harry, returned from settling a small dispute between two tenants, greeted Kent in his normal ebullient manner.

"Aha – come to regale me with your wisdom?" he laughed.

"Had I more of that, I would be far richer than I am now," Kent sighed. "No, I have come to share a thought about this Greatorex fellow."

"I have been far too busy recently to give him more than a passing thought. But I would be happy to hear what thoughts you may have had. I shall pick up a pitcher of ale on my way through to my office."

Seated either side of the desk, a mug of ale in hand, the two sucked off the top froth and grinned at one another.

"Right – Greatorex," Kent started off. "First – he is almost certainly not authorised by anyone in authority. Had he been so, he would have followed up immediately on your refusal to hand over those items. Instead of which, thanks to your tame bloodhounds, he made a circuitous route to a house in Staverton. Your two chaps received the impression that he either owns the place or he is well known to whoever does. So – not anyone in authority, but fully cognizant of the items in question. Let us start from that point – he knows what they are and where they may be found; he has no authority but blandishes a warrant. Conclusions. One - He obtained the warrant by other than proper means. Two – he is after those items either for himself or as an agent for someone else."

"In other words, he is a rogue," Harry grunted.

"Precisely," Kent grunted back. "So – what to do about it? The obvious course is to appraise the sheriff of our conclusions."

"Should we not first find out if he *is* Leonard Greatorex? That could well be an assumed name – assumed to hide his true identity."

"Assumed to protect either himself or to protect any association with a third party that *could* be found via his correct name."

"Before I make any suggestions, I would like your considered opinion of the risks and danger involved," Harry stated.

"Totally unknown, to be absolutely frank. It may not pose any danger at all; on the other hand, it may turn out to be extremely dangerous – depending upon who else is involved – if there is anyone else!"

"And that is my conundrum," Harry growled. "My immediate thought is to send Hob on a mission to find out what he may. Believe me, there is no better ferret in Devon. But I owe him a duty of care, apart from the fact that he is my lifelong friend."

"And if you put it to him?"

"Fatal! He would be off like a scalded cat the moment we had finished speaking. No, I need to think this through carefully before I even broach the subject with him."

"Then I shall leave it with you to do as you think best," Kent nodded.

"Now – what is all this I hear about you and Maud?" Harry gave Kent a knowing grin.

"Is there nothing in this town that remains private?" Kent moaned. "Aye – I have admired her for a while now and have approached the matter as delicately as I could."

"You chose well my friend. Maud is sensible, highly intelligent, and in real need of companionship. But you will have to exercise patience!"

"That I know only too well," Kent acknowledged.

"Believe me, May would to my certain knowledge be delighted if your relationship with her sister blossomed. Mary, needless to say, is in total agreement – as am I."

"Then, with such backing, how may I fail?" Kent finished his ale and rose to leave. He was quite content to leave the matter of Greatorex with the bailiff.

Matthew Kent lived in a large cottage in the town of Bovey Tracey – perhaps, cottage did the dwelling a slight disservice – it was a very *large* cottage. Kent came to collect Maud late on the Saturday morning. He was expecting to find a lady dressed in her Sunday best (although it was Saturday). What he found was a lady dressed in everyday clothes. Maud had taken the view that she wanted to be taken for what she was and not what she looked like.

Nevertheless, Kent was not at all taken aback. In his view, Maud's natural beauty would shine through the meanest dress. He offered her his arm for the short walk down the main street – where their close association was duly noted and reported – and into his very large cottage where his cook/housekeeper had their dinner prepared and waiting for them.

Kent, having been resident for some part of his working life in the corridors of power, was well acquainted with the latest fads and fancies. Therefore, the meal started with a very tasty soup of diced vegetables with crusty bread. This would be followed by a sea bream cooked in almonds, with a side dish of green vegetables, then finished off with a lemon posset. Snowy white linen napkins were placed by the side of each place setting – to be placed over the shoulder for wiping greasy fingers. A white Bordeaux and a deep red Burgundy would accompany the courses. Maud was deeply impressed by the appearance and the taste of entire dinner.

Kent deliberately kept to small talk during the soup, not wanting to press his guest in any way – a fact that also impressed

Maud. Then, as the main fish dish was brought in, she knew that she could prolong the delaying tactics no more.

"Matthew," she set her eating knife at the side of her platter. "You are waiting ever so patiently for my reply to your proposition. For that patience, I would thank you. But I owe you an answer and will keep you in suspense no longer. You will not be surprised to hear that I have consulted my sister. You will not also be surprised to hear that I now am acting upon her advice. Which incidentally tallies entirely with my own feelings. I readily accept that you wish to court me and am happy for you to do so. There!"

"That was quite a speech from someone who is usually spare with her words," Kent gave her a broad smile. "You have no idea how pleased I am to hear them spoken. We are not the usual courting couple – that tends mostly to happen between people of far more tender years. But my intentions are no less ardent and honest than those spoken by mere striplings!"

"Were I not confident of your good intentions, we would not be having this conversation – or even sitting across this table enjoying a rather super dinner," Maud matched his broad smile.

"Then, it behoves me to lay my cards face uppermost upon the table," Kent got serious. "My working life, as you already know, was one of service to what was the parliament under the defunct Commonwealth. I never hounded anyone on their behalf, but I did seek and report upon possible insurrections as and when I discovered them. During those years, I was paid for my services – if not handsomely, then more than was adequate for my living and savings. I am not a poor man – but I do not possess untold riches either. Therefore, I am able to offer you a comfortable and secure life, even if not the ability to cover you in diamonds."

"Believe me," Maud laughed aloud at the idea. "I have never imagined myself bedecked in jewels and finery. A comfortable and secure life is all that I seek. But I insist that I contribute my share towards our expenses. My work with lace is quite remunerative."

"And quite rightly it should be," Kent nodded. "The patterns I have seen you weave are exquisite. Believe me, I am not the sort of man who demands a quiet, domiciled wife. A happy and contented one is far preferrable."

"So, Master Kent, how do you propose going about this courtship – given that we are no longer the mere striplings you mentioned?"

"I propose walks, as and when the weather permits, picnics, hours spent together in conversation – so that we may both get to know one another properly. We are far beyond the age requiring chaperones."

"Indeed, we most certainly are," Maud agreed. "The most important part of that proposition to my mind is that we understand one another fully before you pose the final question. You and I both will be far more able to ask and answer when we are properly aware of one another."

It was at least three hours later when Kent walked Maud back to her home. They had talked quietly at either side of the fireplace until Kent noticed that dusk was setting in. At Maud's gate, he placed a very chaste kiss on Maud's cheek, having arranged a further meeting for a long walk the next day.

CHAPTER XV

Two days later, Harry received a very unexpected visitor. He was appraised of the arrival by the clattering of many hooves. Curious, he himself went to the front door. Then stopped in his tracks as he took in the identity of his caller – plus escort.

Sir Thomas Cartwright had been elected sheriff of Exeter some eighteen months before and had made such an impression with his actions that he had been re-elected when his year had expired. It was indeed the sheriff of the county of Devon who sat astride a large horse, accompanied by a small troop of six soldiers.

"My lord sheriff," Harry gave a small bow. "How may a humble bailiff be of service?"

"I have no need of a humble bailiff," the gruff voice replied. "I have need of a decisive and competent bailiff – and my reports show you to be such a one."

"Then I shall strive not to disappoint," Harry gave a broad grin. "May I invite you to take refreshment. Your soldiers will find adequate refreshment in our kitchens."

The Parke ostler and his junior galloped around to take charge of the horses, to brush them and feed them in the stables. Harry escorted the sheriff into his office, summoning Hob to join him.

Over mugs of excellent ale, the sheriff came immediately to the point of his visit.

"My information is that you have a blighter named Greatorex residing nearby – one who purported to be a representative of the chancellor."

"Purported is exactly the right word, Sir Thomas. My friend, Matthew Kent who is well acquainted with these matters, immediately spotted the discrepancies. Perhaps you should hear from Matthew himself."

Hob was dispatched to fins Kent.

"So, this blighter had the audacity to demand the fruits of your investigation!" Cartwright grunted. "I shall wait upon the arrival

95

of this Master Kent before I proceed further. The tale needs telling just once.”

Kent was ushered in some minutes later and immediately recognised the sheriff. Hob sat quietly at one end of the large desk, pen poised over paper to take notes.

“Right – the items stolen from far and wide,” Cartwright began. “Candlesticks from Rattery, a box from somewhere in Dorset, a dagger and a bag of gold from God alone knows where. This is *not* an isolated happening. Similar discoveries have been made in Honiton, Salisbury, Bath, Tewkesbury and possibly in a host of other places. All the same circumstances – a sack of treasures found apparently abandoned. There are probably far more instances, but never reported. Some thieving buggers are silently blessing their luck at finding such bounty! Yours is certainly not an isolated incident. Now – this sod Greatorex. You say he is hereabouts?”

“My trackers followed him to a small village called Staverton – not many miles distant. As far as I am aware, he is still there. They got the distinct impression that he either owns the house - or is resident there in some capacity.”

“Then we go there immediately and haul the bastard out by his breeches. See what he has to say for himself!”

“I shall summon my trackers to lead us,” Harry nodded.

“And how may you, a country bailiff, have the services of trackers?”

“Oh, that is simply answered, Sir Thomas. They were expert trackers during the conflict between king and parliament. They have worked here ever since.”

“And I may not enquire for which side they did their expert tracking?” Cartwright gave a loud guffaw. “Worry not – it matters not one jot to me. All I ever require is professional expertise.”

Hob was again sent on another jaunt – to find Garvey and Hook. Both were excited at the prospect of joining the venture.

By ten that morning, sheriff, bailiff, assistant bailiff, two trackers and six soldiers clattered out on their short journey to Staverton.

Nell and Kate were enjoying a prolonged stay as guests at the apothecary. Nell watched as Rosie went through her various tasks, questioned possible patients, drew her conclusions. She was deeply impressed - and told James and Avril so.

Not long after the sheriff and his 'posse' had left Parke, another visitor arrived. Adam came riding in from his office in Newton Abbot. One look at his face told Nell that he was not possessed of good news. Over dinner he gave them a brief summary of his findings.

"I spent some days with my father," he said slowly, not relishing what he had to tell. "Suffice it to say that he is determined to pursue this deplorable trade. Not only with his own ships, but with those he gave us for the shipment of granite. He wishes to take possession of our vessels in a week from now. I told him in no uncertain terms that I would never contemplate being a party to this horrible business – and how was I to continue trading the granite from the moor without a ship to my name? Father said that it was of no concern to him – he demanded return of the vessels and, as he had offered me a part in his new enterprise, he had done his duty to me as he saw it. We parted on bitter terms!"

"So, we are without any means of survival from next week?" Nell was aghast.

"It would seem so," Adam nodded. "Thank the Good Lord I had the foresight to hold substantial profits against leaner times. It would seem that they are upon us far sooner that we expected. We *can* survive for many months, but I shall have to use some of those savings to secure us a future by some other means."

"But what of the masters and crews of those three ships? Are they willing to participate in your father's enterprise?"

"One is – the others were appalled at the prospect and declined outright."

"Good for them. Now – are you able to obtain other vessels?" James asked.

"I can comfortably purchase one, but the other two I would have to charter – meaning that a portion of the profit would have to go to whoever owns the vessels. Luckily, that still would leave us in pocket – but not as deeply in pocket were we to own all three."

"So, all is not hopelessly lost?" Nell breathed a sigh of relief.

"No – as far as our future is concerned, all is definitely not lost. But there is a big loss – that of my own father. I shall feel that to my dying day!"

"But is he irretrievably lost to you?" Avril wondered. "Cannot time be a great healer?"

"When he is hell-bent upon an enterprise that I know to be despicable? I fear that the rift cannot be mended."

"You do know that I am one hundred percent in agreement with your detestation of this horrid business?" Nell placed a hand on her husband's.

"Aye, I do – and am heartened beyond measure by it."

"And James and I are also with you," Avril added.

"It is as close to piracy as anything might be," James grated. "They steal people as pirates steal treasure. They live on the profits of their theft just as pirates do. How can any king or government not see the evil that is lining their coffers?"

"Oh, simply indeed," Adam gave a saddened glance at the person he regarded as his father-in-law – even though Nell was *not* James' daughter. "The royal coffers would welcome funds from any source – even from the sale of human beings!"

It was about the dinner hour when the sheriff and his company arrived at the small village of Staverton. They had approached it via the villages of Ipplepen and Broadhempston. Sir Thomas stopped well before the ancient bridge that spanned the river Dart, and out of sight of the houses. He called the two trackers forward.

"Point out for me the house," he said.

Hook pointed to the second, rather large house on the right of the lane, just around a left bend in the road.

"Good – now, one of you take three of my soldiers and get to the rear of that house – without being seen. I shall wait for fifteen minutes before I approach the front. My men with you will deal with anyone attempting to flee out the back."

Garvey and Hook went through their usual, and totally unique, way of deciding who did what. It consisted of eyebrows and winks. Garvey dismounted and led three soldiers on foot into a small wood on their left. A few minutes later came the very distinct call of a wood pigeon – repeated three times.

"He's in position," Hook reported quietly.

Sir Thomas consulted a large pocket watch and waited. He addressed Harry, Hob and his other three soldiers quietly.

"Right – we ride up to the house as noisily as you like. We dismount and hammer on the door. Be prepared to answer fire. Draw pistols and have them ready cocked."

Harry and Hob looked at one another and decided to follow on in the rear, neither being in possession of a firearm.

All was sudden movement. Sir Thomas led the gallop to the house, dismounted and stalked to the front door, upon which he hammered with the iron hilt of a wicked looking dagger.

"I order you to open this door in the name of the king!" he bellowed. Silence was the only response.

"People moving inside the house – top floor, right window," came another bellow from the rear of the property.

Sir Thomas raised his voice another notch.

"Last chance to answer the door. Fail to do so and it will be forced!"

There were only three other houses in the row. Three doors opened, three heads poked out, took in the scene of an angry sheriff and armed soldiers, and promptly went back inside to the sound of bolts being slid into place.

The sheriff turned to one of his soldiers. "Fetch that rope from my saddlebag and bring it to me."

He then went to the window of the downstairs room on the left of the door and, using the hilt of his dagger again, smashed a diamond of glass between the lead cames, the one nearest to the inner catch. He fed the rope through the hole and tied it to the iron catch. He and one soldier than heaved on the rope – the window burst open outwards.

Without any further orders, two of the soldiers went through the window. Then came the sound of bolts being withdrawn as the front door was opened.

The sheriff and his one remaining soldier dashed straight in, the four of them scouring the ground floor. They found nobody. All four congregated in the hall, well out of the way of any pistols being fired down the stairs. Once again, Sir Thomas resorted to a stentorian bellow.

"Whoever you are up there, come down now and surrender. You have five minutes, or we shall come up ready to fire upon anyone we find."

There came a sudden flurry of movement as a small, elderly woman descended the stairs. Holding firmly to the banister. She halted at the bottom step and peered back down the hall.

"I am alone in this house, whoever you are. You have scared a poor old woman half to death!"

"Madam, you have nothing to fear from us," the sheriff suddenly became urbane and mannerly. "Just come here to me and I shall explain everything."

The old woman descended the last step and walked to Sir Thomas.

"My name, madam, is Thomas Cartwright, sheriff of Devon. I have reason to believe that a certain Master Greatorex is residing here. He is someone I need to question. So, if he *is* here, pray call him down now."

"I have already stated that I am alone here," came the somewhat haughty reply.

One of the soldiers from the rear came into the hall, having run down the side of the house.

"Load of bollocks, my lord," he announced.

"How very uncouth!" the lady interrupted.

"Seriously, my lord, there is more movement from up above."

"Then it seems we must go up and see for ourselves," Sir Thomas almost gave a wolfish grin. "Tell whoever it is that we will come up, fire first and ask questions second."

The old lady gave a resigned shrug and raised her voice. "Leonard, you had better come down. I have no wish to see my only son killed."

"And why were you both hiding up there?" the sheriff asked.

"Armed soldiers arrive unannounced, hammer upon my door – what else do you expect an old woman and her peace-loving son to do but hide?"

Leonard chose that moment to come down the stairs, his hands held well away from his body. Two soldiers grabbed him and frisked him for weapons. One pistol, one large dagger, and a smaller knife clattered onto the floor.

"It is like my mother explained," he said. "We reacted as any other innocent people would have – we hid from violence."

"Then you have nothing to fear from answering my questions, have you?"

"As an innocent, peaceable citizen, I have nothing of interest to tell you."

"Bailiff!" roared Sir Thomas.

Harry, with Hob in tow, appeared at the front door.

"Master Bailiff – can you identify this man?"

"Certainly, I can Sir Thomas. Some time past, he came to Parke showing me a warrant. He said that his name was Leonard Greatorex and that he had authority to take possession of certain very valuable items."

"Search again!" the sheriff ordered.

A somewhat crumpled warrant came to light from the innermost pocket of the tunic.

"Explain!" the sheriff barked, waving the warrant under the nose of a now dejected Greatorex.

"Oh, Leonard – what have you done?" the old lady looked on the point of collapse.

"The first thing I shall need to know is how you managed to obtain this," the sheriff put the warrant into his wallet. "And then we will really get down to the meat of the matter – how you knew of the items. You will be taken immediately to the nearest stronghold – probably Totnes castle. And then we shall begin a long and interesting talk. Madam – it would appear that your son has been involved in something of which you were not cognisant. Our apologies for the manner of our entry. This should cover the cost of the repair to your window."

He placed a small, gold coin on the hall table and went back outside. Greatorex, held firmly between two soldiers, was marched outside and tied by the wrists to the pommel of a saddle. Everyone mounted up and started the short journey across the bridge, through Dartington, to Totnes castle. He was deposited into a cell.

Sir Thomas, Harry, Hob and the soldiers then went in search of a very late dinner.

"I am likely to be here for some time," Harry said to Hob. "Ride back home and tell Mary she is not to worry and that I shall be back either later today, or tomorrow."

Even in early February, the large double doors of the smithy were propped wide open. The heat from the forge could even be felt by people passing up the road. Two men were busy fashioning iron rods into a new gate for the bakery next door, the old one having rusted away. One man, in his mid-thirties, could easily have been a giant of old. He wielded his hammer as if it were merely a spoon. The younger man, nearly eighteen, held the red-hot rod over the anvil for his father to shape. Simon Smith was in his element, noting that he no longer had to give any instruction to his son Jack. Jack was never going to assume the gigantic proportions of either his father or grandfather Abel. Nevertheless, he easily outweighed any other young man in the town. He held his end of the rod in a wad of sacking, noted that it was getting dull, then removed it, to place it again in the forge, using one hand to operate the bellows lever.

"Only a further nine to do," he grinned as the rod was again placed on the anvil.

"This is the last we shall do this side of dinner," Simon grunted, hammering the end into a flat surface that would be used as a tongue to be fixed into place in a slot in the top rail of the gate.

"Is mother giving us more of that pork stew?" Jack asked as he plunged the flattened end into a bucket of water.

"That, my son, is my fondest wish," Simon grinned. "Hungry?"

"Am I ever anything else?" Jack grinned back.

His sister them came through from the house, through the door that led straight from the smithy into their parlour. Rachael had recovered from her adventure with the bogus letter, but breathed fire and brimstone at the mere mention of Will and Peterkin.

"Mother says that you need wash for dinner," she announced. Imelda added her own comment from the doorway.

"And wash all the grime off this time, if you please!"

Using another bucket of clean water, father and son removed flakes of ash from face and hands, wiped themselves dry on a piece of towelling and were about to follow Rachael into the parlour when Jack espied a slight figure walking up to the tavern.

"I shall be just a moment," he said, galloping off in pursuit. Father and daughter exchanged a grin as Jack sped off after Rosie.

Jack easily caught up with Rosie, who was delivering a jar of ointment to a traveller who was staying at the tavern.

"I have a mind to take a walk along the river this evening after work," Jack said, falling in at Rosie's side. "Would you care to accompany me?"

Rosie stood and faced the young man squarely and prepared to deliver a stern lecture.

"Jack – who is your father?" she enquired.

Jamie knew where this was going. "You know as well as I who is my father," he muttered.

"And who is the sister of your father? My own mother! And that makes us cousins. Whatever notion has been boiling in that head of yours is sheer nonsense. Listen carefully, Jack – there can never be any relationship between the two of us other than cousins!"

And with that, Rosie strode onwards. Jack shuffled his feet and walked disconsolately back.

Jamie rode carefully to Brimley, carefully because he was riding a horse with which he was not familiar. It was quite a lot bigger than his normal mount; this one stood close to sixteen hands and had a look in its eye that said, 'muck me about and I'll have you off in a trice!' Hence, Jamie was riding slowly and very carefully.

He arrived eventually at Brimley and, very gratefully, handed the horse over to the stable hand. He went into the manor in search of Colonel Larkin. He found him in the large study. Arranged on the table were the map that Jamie had laboriously marked and annotated, plus the reams of notes he had written.

Larkin glanced up from his desk and gave Jamie a cheery wave.

"Thank you for coming," he said. "I wanted us to get the next stage of exploration clear in our minds – not that we shall start until after Easter. Too damned cold up there."

Jamie went over to the map and reminded himself where they had spent the autumn and early winter of the previous year.

"We covered a very large area, centred upon Holne," he said, tracing their pervious meandering route with his finger.

"And I thought that we could move north from there – into a large triangle from Buckland, north to Widecombe, then south-west to Dartmeet,"

Jamie traced that area. On the map, it looked small indeed. But as an area to search and map, it was anything but small.

"It's going to take us months to complete that," he ventured.

"Indeed, it is," Larkin nodded. "But we do not have to do it all without a break. I suggest that we spend three weeks at a time up there, followed by one week back here for making reports, entering references, and sorting through our finds."

That sounded to Jamie like a very good idea. Three weeks on the moor and one week in the manor house – eating like a lord.

"I wonder what we may find this time? I doubt we shall find another item that is of interest to the king!"

"No, that was exceptional. We cannot expect to do that every time."

"Shall I make a start planning our first route?" Jamie asked.

"Aye – you do that. We now have a good idea how much ground we may cover in a week. Plan for the first three and let me have your findings."

"My pleasure, master," Jamie sat down and made an enthusiastic start.

The Reverend James Forbes sat gazing into the flames that danced over the split ash logs in the grate. He sat with a glass of wine in one hand – a glass that he had filled some time previously and from which he had yet to take the first sip. He tried to conjure up the face of his old friend Colonel Fisher but was confused at the many versions that appeared. Fisher had been many people, each with a separate expression. There had been the bluff old army colonel, the irascible denouncer of Cromwell and the parliamentary associates, the voluble supporter of this appalling slave trade, the man who could bellow with mirth at lewd jokes – to name but a very few.

News had reached the rectory just after Forbes had finished his dinner – news delivered by the old servant that Fisher had retained after his retirement. The old colonel had simply fallen asleep in his chair after breaking his fast and had simply passed away in that same sleep. Forbes was a sad man.

Nearly fifty-three years of age, Forbes had lived a varied existence. He had been, as a younger man, chaplain to the then Prince of Wales – now king Charles II. Unceremoniously removed by parliament from his 'living' in Bovey Tracey – presumably because of that previous, 'royal' connection, he had been formally reinstated in 1661 when a king once again sat on England's (and Scotland's) throne. During his life, he had made many friends. Fisher was probably the most memorable of them. William Garlick, his long-time churchwarden, dead some years past. Then the living friends – James and Avril Ramsey, Peter and Laura Cove – retired bailiff and wife; Luke and Grace Barton – steward at Parke and still going strong. So many good and trustworthy people.

Fisher had expressed a wish that his funeral be held at Bovey Tracey, and that he be interred in the nearby cemetery. Forbes would honour those wishes. There had been an informal 'club' called The Sane And Sensible – members Forbes, Fisher, Larkin, and Kent. That was now down to three. Forbes entertained the notion of proposing a replacement but would air his thoughts first to the remaining other two members. How would they react to his proposal? Even in the depths of gloom, this raised a smile to his face. At last, he raised his glass to his old friend and took that first sip.

It was just after dinner that Will rounded on his twin. Their meagre dinner had been taken sitting on the wall of the pigsty. Their banishment was still in operation, despite Will's constant badgering of their father to relent. Harry was still furious with them.

"You were never really behind me, were you?" Will groused.

"No, not entirely. It seemed to be petty and a bit cruel," Peterkin admitted.

"Then why did you not make a more forceful argument against it? We would not be in this mess if you had persuaded me!"

"Because we are brothers – and twins, although you are my senior by fifteen minutes. You never cease to remind me of that fact!"

"Then, because I am older than you, you see the need to agree with anything I say!"

"No – that is not what I am saying. I frequently disagree with you, but I go along simply to keep the peace between us."

"So, you admit to being weak minded?"

"Will – are you deliberately attempting to cause a rift between us? I disagree with almost every scheme you dream up. They are always fraught with difficulty and are often thoughtless and cruel."

"And yet, in your weakness of character, you simply go along with them to keep the peace?"

"If that is what you choose to believe. And stop asking Lauren to intervene with our father. It is not fair on our sister!"

"Sisters, like all girls, are put on this earth to serve us men!"

"That is a stupid remark – and I believe that you know it is. For once in your life, Will, stop behaving like a spoilt child. We did wrong and everyone in the whole town knows we did wrong. Simply accept it and show a bit of remorse."

"That Rachael is a stuck-up cow! Just because her father is as strong as an ox does not make her any less worthy of being humbled."

"Apart from that," Peterkin had not finished. "You humiliated Billy. He is a simple-minded lad and did not deserve what happened to him. It is as I said – cruel."

"Then I shall take it that you wish to dissociate yourself from anything I do in future – as you regard me as cruel."

Peterkin heaved a sigh. "Will – you must take my remarks any way you choose. I am ashamed of what we did. Apparently, you are not. Let us leave it at that.

Later that same afternoon, Sir Thomas started to question Leonard Greatorex. The man had been brought up from his cell and sat on a stool facing an irate sheriff. Harry sat at the side of the room, whilst two soldiers stood behind the prisoner.

"The first question is simply this," the sheriff began. "How did you obtain the warrant that you showed to Master Bailiff. It is patently obvious that nobody in authority handed it to you. So – where and how did you obtain it?"

Greatorex glared at the sheriff and kept his mouth closed.

"By your silence, I must assume that you obtained it by false means." Harry was very surprised at the sheriff's quiet voice. He would have expected shouting and swearing. "Then, assuming you obtained it by false means, I charge you with treason. It bears the seal of the Lord Chancellor, who is the representative of the king. To claim authority to which you are not entitled is treason. And you are aware of the penalty for that crime."

Harry was hardly surprised to see Greatorex swallow nervously. He *was* surprised at what followed.

"I get the distinct impression that you, Leonard Greatorex, are a mere pawn in this affair – a lowly functionary in a scheme that is far bigger than you purport to be. Therefore, I shall have you returned to your cell. Think long and hard during the night on what I have just said – treason against the king and his ministers is punishable via the most horrible of means. Think very hard! I shall question you again in the morning."

After the man had been marched out, Harry turned a questioning face to Sir Thomas.

"You seem surprised that I did not immediately start to wreak havoc upon his most private parts!" he chortled.

"Well, I did wonder," Harry admitted.

"This whole business stinks to high heaven – and I am positive that this idiot's part is but a small cog in a much larger wheel. The best course is to let his imagination dwell upon what may well befall him. We shall see!"

CHAPTER XVI

Two days later, James and Avril again received a visit from Nell. She had ridden to Bovey Tracey in company with a family of thatchers, who had heard of a cottage for rent on the Heath.

"More news?" Avril gave Nell a hug as she removed her very warm riding cloak.

"Yes, more news," Nell gave a hug in return. "And this time, news of a far more positive nature."

"It shall have to wait until dinner, I am afraid," Avril pouted. "James and I are inundated with requests for that linctus to soothe sore throats – of which there seem to be far more than usual. Rosie is due back soon from delivering a basket full. She may wish to impart news of her own."

"Oh – news of a personal nature?"

"Indeed so!"

"Then, it is not before time," Nell laughed.

"That, James and I would heartily agree. Now, let me make use of your undoubted talents and ask you to pound up another batch of rose hips. My arm is aching from the pestle and mortar!"

Rosie arrived back just before dinner, which because of the turmoil in the apothecary workroom, was a simple affair of the remains of the previous day's mutton stew.

"Well, the news?" James prompted.

Nell was almost bubbling over with excitement and had to compose herself so as to render the information in the correct order.

"Adam has severed all business relationship with his father, and as a consequence, lost all three ships to this new, vicious trade. Only one master and crew went with the ships, so that his father has had to recruit new masters and crews for the other two vessels. Adam has chartered two vessels so that our own business of ferrying granite may carry on. He has also obtained an option to purchase the ships when profits from the trade allow. The two masters and crews who remained loyal to him are tending to these chartered vessels. Admittedly, our trade has suffered a one-third reduction, but it will not be for too long. Adam is sure that we will be up to full strength before too many months have passed."

Both James and Avril heaved sighs of relief at this news.

"So, the savings from profits are being spent partly on the charter?" James asked.

"Indeed so," Nell nodded. "But with granite being in such demand for the rebuilding of London, the cost of charter is but a small dent into the over-all profit. All things considered, we have come through the horrid affair reasonably intact. I still maintain my own small business – and that has helped in maintaining our fair way of life."

"And how is your own health – considering that you have not *that* long to go before Kate gets a little brother or sister?" Avril asked.

"My health, dearest mama, is excellent. I expect little one to start kicking and making his presence felt very soon."

"And now, I have some news for you, Nell," Rosie gave a shy smile.

"Oh – you have discovered a cure for leprosy? A way to banish all sickness?" Nell grinned.

"Actually, no. I am holding back on those until I can be assured of my fortune," Rosie quipped back. "My news concerns something slightly more mundane than earth-shattering discoveries. Some days past, Jack proposed taking me on a walk. At first, I could not believe what he was implying – we are cousins of the nearest possible kind. When I reminded him of that fact, he seemed taken aback – almost as if he could not see that as any impediment to our future relationship. I shall have to speak to Uncle Simon and Aunt Imelda as I am sure that they do not know of his infatuation."

"Do your own mother and father know of this?" Nell asked.

"No, I have yet to tell them."

"Then I would suggest that you tell all of them together. Can Jack really be that insensitive?"

"Well, I for one would never have believed so," Avril stated.

"And no more would I have," James agreed with a shake of his head.

Kent was surprised when Sir Thomas decided to keep Greatorex in suspense for yet another day. Harry, unable to stay away from his duties as bailiff, reluctantly rode back to Bovey, but only with the assurance that Kent would keep him appraised of any discoveries.

Once again, Greatorex was marched into the bare room. On his stool, he was not the same man who had been brought to Totnes castle. He was dishevelled, unwashed, unkempt. He looked completely downcast.

"I trust you have been giving due thought to your predicament," the sheriff growled at him. "So, Master Greatorex, I *will* have the truth from you. Start talking!"

"Little else has occupied my mind," Greatorex mumbled.

"Thought it may be the case," Sir Thomas gave a grunt of satisfaction. "So, what have you to tell me?"

"Believe it or not, theft was *not* the main reason for the removal of those precious items," Greatorex was spinning out his explanation. He had come to the conclusion that, if he were to *slowly* release his information, his inquisitor would see him in a more kindly light.

"If not theft, then what was the purpose?" the sheriff growled. "Bear in mind that, whatever the underlying purpose, theft *was* committed!"

Greatorex had thought out his plan of revelation very carefully. He needed to enlist understanding.

"Tell me, my Lord Sheriff – what think you of the state of law and order under this king? Is it good – in that proper order is maintained? Or is it lax – where licentiousness, permissiveness, and downright evil is dismissed with scarcely a remark? Many in this land think the latter – and not without very good reason. One such is a gentleman who lives in Dorset. He became so enraged at the conduct of those in command that he determined to demonstrate that law and order could be set aside with barely a thought."

The sheriff refrained from comment for a moment as he digested all this.

"Are you telling me that this person – who you have yet to name – *engineered* these thefts simply to make a point?"

"Exactly that," Greatorex replied. "And it is certainly not confined to Devon and Dorset. There have been over one hundred similar acts throughout the length and breadth of England."

Sir Thomas had been aware of a few more in Devon, but certainly nothing on this scale. What had he not been told by those in authority?

"Well, you now have got my undivided attention," he grunted. "As you have gone so far already, let us have the rest."

"Then let me place the full facts before you so that you may see the justice of the plan. This gentleman – who I shall name – devised a plan where people of note and importance were relieved temporarily of their prized possessions. They would, obviously, rant and rave at the inability of those in charge to put a stop to it. When the time was right, this gentleman would then see that all property was returned to its rightful owners whilst, at the same time, make it widely known that the government was useless, concentrating solely upon their lives of pleasure. To that end, he was able to obtain a copy of the correct seal to affix to the warrants that he gave to his agents – one of whom I am proud to be. My aim in demanding possession of the items was *not* to make profit from them but to return them to their owners. I am *not* a thief!"

"And how do you describe a man who takes what is not his?"

"No better – or no worse – than a man of government who takes taxes from hard-pressed workers so that it may be spent upon debauchery by those in command!"

Sir Thomas paused. He was an honest man and had often harboured unkindly thoughts about a court hell-bent upon a life of pleasure. However, he was still a sheriff.

"Even so, that man is a thief, no matter what the motivation. The removal of property without authorisation is theft – pure and simple."

"Even if the purpose is simply to borrow the items to make a point?"

"No matter the reason! Now – down to brass tacks. Who is this person?"

"His name is Templeton – Lord Herbert Templeton. A brave and dedicated upholder of law and order."

That rang a very loud bell.

"But he was one whose property was taken!"

"Donated to the cause!"

"And he has over a hundred like you doing his bidding?"

"I hope, more successful than I have been. I had no idea that I had been discovered."

"Thanks to the eagle eye of an ex-parliamentary agent and the assistance of very experienced trackers. Now back to you. You shall be held here until it is determined how matters are to proceed. You will be kept secure, but not in a cell. You will be fed properly. I shall need you alive and healthy to relate all this to others – others who are far above me in the chain of command."

It was just before dinner when the town of Bovey Tracey was aware that all was not well opposite the church. Flames were shooting out of the windows and door of the bakery which stood on the opposite side of the road.

The two apprentices, plus the young lad who lived and worked there were hurling buckets of water through the doorway in a somewhat futile attempt to quench the flames. Gerald Shooter, the baker, was hardly helping matters by standing apart and screaming often contradictory orders.

Simon and Jack from the next-door smithy galloped over with more buckets but realised that putting this conflagration out was but a forlorn hope. Many others from nearby shops and houses joined in the throng.

After a half-hour of frantic efforts, the fire was at last finished its work. The bakery itself was a charred mess, although the house behind it had miraculously escaped serious damage.

Thirty or so people stood and surveyed the wreckage, wiping soot and smuts from faces and clothes. Gerald Shooter was still screaming.

"It is all the fault of the smith," he bellowed. "Stray sparks must have ignited the roof."

"That is a load of hogwash," Simon retorted. "There is a distance of at least forty yards from our furnace to the roof of the bakery. A spark would have cooled by the time it had travelled half that distance."

"I demand that you be arrested for causing the fire," Shooter screamed. "My business is now lying in ruins thanks to your criminal acts!"

Harry, summoned by the ever-vigilant Hob, arrived at a run.

"Bailiff – arrest this arsonist," Shooter yelled.

"And why should I do that?" Harry asked.

"The baker claims that a spark from the smithy started the fire," one helpful neighbour explained.

"And I maintain that that could not happen. Look – I shall demonstrate what I mean," Simon spoke in a reasonable voice. "Jack, run into the house and fetch some pieces of paper."

Jack came back with three sheets which Simon handed out, one to the bailiff, one to the neighbour, and kept one himself.

"Now – fetch that iron bar from the furnace and hammer it as hard as you can – send the sparks this way and we shall all endeavour to catch them on our paper."

One iron bar, by then almost white hot, was hammered, causing a shower of sparks to fly towards the three men.

"There – what did I tell you!" Simon held up his paper on which were barely discernible marks.

Harry and the neighbour did likewise.

"See – and we were no more than fifteen yards from the anvil!" Simon explained.

"Some sparks landed on my hand – and they were barely even hot," the neighbour spoke up. "Whatever caused this fire, twas certainly not the smithy!"

"You shall pay dearly for this!" Shooter glared at Simon. "I shall have my revenge on you!"

Harry immediately stepped between the baker and the massive smith. Had he not done so, a severely damaged baker would have resulted.

"You shall do no such thing," Harry waved an admonitory finger at Shooter. "We have all witnessed the fact that the smithy is not to blame. I advise you to look nearer to home for the culprit!"

One of the two apprentices took a step forward.

"Master, that oven door has not been closing properly for some weeks now. Could not the stray spark not have escaped from it?"

"My equipment can *not* be at fault. Someone must have set the fire deliberately. Perhaps one of you did it!" He advanced on the three employees menacingly.

"But why would we deliberately endanger our own livelihood?" the young man asked, not unreasonably.

"I shall have the truth from you even if I have to beat it from your mouths!" Shooter bellowed.

Again, Harry interposed himself between baker and employees. "Once again, Master Shooter, I shall not allow that to happen. You would do well to retire to your house and we will inspect the damage when it has cooled sufficiently."

"You may not stand between a master and his employees!" Shooter snarled.

"Strange to relate, that is precisely what I am doing," Harry said, calling on his supply of patience. "Go indoors and cool yourself off!"

"You three are dismissed from my employ," Shooter hissed at the three. The little lad was near to tears, whilst the two apprentices merely shrugged.

"I am willing to wager that your own oven was responsible," the neighbour faced Shooter. "You were always a miserable, penny-pinching wretch. Dear God, we mourn the departure of John and Evelyn. They were good people and fair employers – and their bread was far superior to yours!"

That caused a ripple of agreement from everyone else. That caused Harry to think about what had just been said.

"Tell me, Master Shooter," he said quietly. "Would you consider selling the house? You cannot sell the bakehouse as it has ceased to be such."

"I would be very glad to shake the dust of this wretched town from my feet. I have been subjected to abuse ever since I came here."

"And every word of it justified," came another voice.

Shooter stalked back into his house – via the back door. Harry shooed everyone away, and the three lads to the tavern where he knew Sal would take care of them. He walked back to Parke eager to speak to Mary about her parents, John and Evelyn Ramsey.

Kent arrived back at Parke in the mid-afternoon. He immediately sought out Harry to regale him with the news from Totnes.

"And this was simply a stunt to demonstrate the ineptitude of government?" Harry queried.

"It would appear so – and I have no doubts about the story that Greatorex related. He seemed almost proud to have been chosen to be a part of it."

"I know that many people feel disillusioned by this king and his court's display of debauchery – which he would appear to condone," Harry spoke carefully. "But surely this is not the way to go about a remedy."

"Indeed not," Kent agreed. "But I feel compelled to see some justification in the action. What is reportedly going on at court is a disgrace. A queen shamed, a gaggle of mistresses and their illicit offspring paraded without let or hindrance. The chief officers of state seem to be powerless to alter things – and that powerlessness is regarded as complicity. But still and all, this plan is not the way to alter the situation. I fear for the lives of all concerned!"

"He is being referred to as The Merry Monarch," Harry thought aloud. "But how may merrymaking be allowed to go to these lengths?"

"They should not!" Kent stated. "We are going to hear more about this ill-conceived plan – and may be called upon to play some further part."

CHAPTER XVII

The month of March had come in like a roaring lion, gales swept down from the moor, rain lashed every surface, rivers were swollen and, in some cases, had flooded neighbouring land to a depth of two or three feet. The area around Teingrace, long known as a floodplain, served that purpose as it had done for centuries past.

Gil and Ella looked out every morning to see what damage had been done to their many rows of vegetables. But Bovey Heath was well drained, so they had escaped quite lightly.

And then, as suddenly as it had begun, the period of gales and rain ceased, bringing sunshine and a degree of warmth. It was on the second morning of this welcome change that Adam, Nell, and Kate arrived for another visit to James and Avril. During the break for dinner, Adam brought the Ramseys up to date with progress.

"We now have our two chartered vessels working and are negotiating the hire of a third," Adam began. "All of our trips are between here in Devon and London, so each trip takes a vessel very little time. We have also had a stroke of luck. Instead of returning empty as fast as possible for the next load, both of our vessels are returning loaded with a variety of goods from many merchants – tobacco, ironware, cloth. The return journey takes longer what with loading and unloading these goods, but the profits have almost doubled. All in all, we have come out of that horrid mess relatively unscathed."

"Adam says that, when we acquire the third vessel, he will have to take on a young clerk to help with the books. Adam acts as his own dockmaster, supervising cargoes, loading and unloading. A third vessel will leave him very little time for the essential work with the tallies and the ledgers."

"And Mama is teaching me to read and write," little Kate added. "And to make cakes and soup!"

"Then you are going to be a huge help," Avril noted. "Especially when your little brother arrives."

"But it might be a tiny sister," Kate objected. "I shall help change her and read her stories, and keep her safe, and put her to bed."

"So, what with your help in the kitchen- and with this new little one – you are going to be a very busy little girl," James grinned at her.

"And have you spoken to yours and Jack's parents?" Nell asked Rosie.

"I have not yet had the opportunity. But I shall have to as it cannot be allowed to rest as it is!"

Paul Larkin, ex-colonel of the old parliamentary army, had received a letter some days previously, a letter that had him scratching his head. It was very official, set about with seals and elaborate, bureaucratic wording. In essence, he was 'invited' to attend at court to receive the official thanks of the king. That kind of invitation was definitely a royal command!

Highly intrigued, he had packed a valise and had ridden to Westminster to arrive the day before his 'invitation'. Dressed in his best outfit, he presented himself at a large double doorway, showing his letter to the officer in charge of the two sentries. This officer preceded Larkin into a huge room and announced him to a very grand man seated behind a desk that could have served as a banqueting table for fifty people.

He had expected to be greeted by Edward Hyde, the Lord Chancellor. The man behind the huge desk was not Hyde. The man, swathed in robes of various hues, rose and gestured Larkin to a seat opposite.

"I am very pleased to meet you," he said, extending a hand that contained a ring on each finger, but not on the thumb. "Arlington," he prompted.

"Aha," Larkin thought. "Henry Bennet, first Earl Arlington – secretary of state."

"I am honoured to meet you, my lord," he said aloud.

"You are no doubt wondering why you have been summoned to meet his majesty," Arlington could not supress a grin of mischief. "Let me enlighten you. The king is ever aware of the legacy of his father - a king done to death by the very parliament that you served. Have no fear – this is not at all related to your years of service. It is solely to do with the badge that you discovered and returned, very properly I might add, to his majesty. Not that many have survived. His own, of course; one presented to my colleague Lord Clarendon; one recovered from the effects of Prince Rupert. There were many others that have not survived, until you retrieved the one that had been presented to Lord Hopton. So, you may readily appreciate that the king is extremely grateful for both the finding and the honest return. I can well imagine that another finder would have not been so forthcoming. I can now tell you that the king has a reward that he feels in keeping with such honest service. Beyond that, my lips are sealed!"

"Ye Gods," Larkin thought. "What manner of reward can it be. Jamie and I already shared a large purse!"

"I am indeed honoured, my lord," he managed.

"Now, we shall proceed from here through a few other rooms to the presence chamber. Pray follow me."

Larkin, in a sort of daze, followed behind Lord Arlington through three rooms, each larger than the preceding one, and each peopled by groups of men and women in rising order of importance. Finally, they were admitted to the presence chamber, at the far end of which sat King Charles II on an immense, golden throne. It was set upon a raised dais. In front of the dais was a very small, low padded stool. Arlington paused and executed an elaborate bow.

"Your majesty, may I present Master Paul Larkin," he announced. Larkin followed suit with just as elaborate a bow.

To his surprise, the king stood up and went to the front of the dais.

"Come forward so that I may see you clearly," he almost lisped. That was, unbeknown to Larkin, becoming a new habit of the court – an affectation that was supposed to differentiate the upper orders from the lower orders.

Larkin, still in a bit of a daze, did as ordered. The king reached into a side pocket of his richly brocaded frock coat and brought out a wrapping of linen. He opened the linen into the palm of his left hand to expose four badges.

"These are of great significance to me," he said, almost to himself. "I had but three – mine, my brother James' Duke of York, and that of cousin Rupert. Because of your honesty, Master Lakin, I now possess four. I fear that I shall never be in possession of any others. I also understand that you were against me during the wars with parliament."

"Yes, sire – I was. First as a sergeant of infantry, then as a captain of horse, finally a colonel."

"Then you must have been a singularly effective soldier to rise so far. Cromwell, may his soul rot in hell, was ever cautious with his promotions. But despite your opposition to me – and I will not enquire where and how that opposition was manifested – you found and returned to me something that you knew you were not at liberty to keep for yourself!"

"Theft, your majesty, is theft – no matter the nature of the stolen item or its value. I could not in all conscience keep it as a memento."

"Then I am confirmed in what I intended to do," the king nodded to himself. "Sergeant, your sword." He turned to one of the sentries standing guard at either side of the massive throne. "Come, Master Larkin – kneel on the stool."

Either he is about to make me knight or lop my head off, Larkin thought as he bent his knees to kneel on the low stool. He felt the lightest touch on either shoulder.

"And now arise, Sir Paul Larkin, with the thanks of your king. Master Gafney," he turned again to a clerk who was sat at a far table. "Prepare the necessary papers and present them to me for my seal. Sir Paul – go with My Lord Arlington. The necessary paper of your appointment will be with you shortly."

In a state of some confusion, Larkin stood, said words of thanks and remembered to retreat three paces before following Arlington from the presence chamber.

It was the following day when Kent and Harry were summoned to Exeter. They were to attend and bear witness at the upcoming trial of Greatorex. A special court of assize was being set in motion. Someone, somewhere, thought Kent, had thought it of sufficient importance to bring this about so speedily.

The two duly arrived at the large guildhall the next morning. They were met by Sir Thomas.

"Do not register surprise when you see the magnitude of the proceedings," the sheriff warned them. "As you are well aware from that stupid man's story, his is by no means an isolated case!"

Kent and Harry were shown into a side room to await being called into court. They were but two of many sitting around the walls on padded benches. A court official called for their attention.

"Gentlemen – I have to instruct you not to talk about the various cases to which you will be called for evidence. By all means discuss the weather, the state of the last harvest, even the colour of your ladies' latest fashions. But do *not* discuss the matters before the court."

The men introduced themselves to one another – that being permissible. There were seven places represented. Bovey, Dorchester, Plymouth, Devizes, Bath, Launceston, and Barnstaple. Had a theft occurred in each of those places, Kent wondered?

It was gone nine in the morning when Harry was called. He followed the usher into the huge hall that had been set up as the court. Facing him was an elderly judge of assize – sitting alone behind a desk raised upon a dais. Various legal people sat at desks in the body of the court. Looking over his shoulder, Harry noted a railed-off area where seven people were sitting – guarded by soldiers. One of them was Greatorex.

Harry was shown to a lectern where an official ministered the oath. One of the stern legal types rose and addressed him.

"Master Cove – are you bailiff to the Parke Estate and did you have a matter of discovery brought to your attention?"

"Yes, sir. I am and I did."

"Please tell the court what occurred."

Harry launched into his explanation of the discovery and his immediate investigation – from discovering ownership of the candlesticks to the name in the box.

"And did you subsequently receive a visit from one of the persons sitting in the accused section?"

Harry again went through the visit by Greatorex, the following of him and the discovery of his whereabouts. He identified Greatorex.

Sitting on a bench at the back of the court, Harry witnessed the evidence given by Kent, then by the sheriff himself.

"And the name of Templeton was given freely by this man?"

"Indeed so, sir."

Greatorex was then brought forward by two burly guards and asked whether what had been said was a true account. He looked downcast as he muttered that it was.

The judge looked up and glared at Greatorex.

"You have pleaded guilty to theft. I remand you into the custody of my lord sheriff until such time as I shall pass sentence. Take him away."

It took the rest of that day and all of the following day to get through the other six. All pleaded guilty to similar thefts. All were remanded. The judge them pronounced what was to follow.

"Sufficient evidence has been heard to justify a warrant for the arrest of Lord Templeton. This matter is far from completed. My summary shall be sent to the Lord Chief Justice and will form a substantial part of the evidence at that trial. In the meantime, I require the seven accused back here to receive sentence."

Just before court rose for the day, all seven were given sentences of transportation for life to a penal colony that nobody had ever heard of. Harry and Kent went back home the next morning with tales to relate.

Mary had come up with an idea. Even she was the first to admit that it was radical in the extreme. The first thing she did was to visit her parents – John and Evelyn – to sound them out. If they had said no, then the whole idea would have been dead in the water. However, they did not say no. Therefore, Mary waited impatiently for Harry to return. She would never have dreamed of going ahead without first sounding out her husband. Not only was Harry her partner in life, he was also the bailiff.

Ever since Shooter had disappeared – almost literally in a cloud of smoke – various people throughout the small town had started baking bread. But this was not something that could continue. What was needed was a proper bakery. Every town had at least one, as did every village.

The two apprentices and the young lad had been on hand to help out so that most people got bread on most days. The situation with the lads was yet another thing that could not last indefinitely – hence Mary's impatience to get her idea accepted.

Harry listened with growing interest as Mary propounded her idea. He thought it a brilliant solution. The very next morning after his return, he and Hob posted notices saying that a very important meeting would be held in the church that very evening – and that everyone *should* attend. Reverend Forbes, appraised in advance, thought it a superb idea.

The church was packed that evening, children sat on parents' knees; younger members stood packed together in the aisles. Reverend Forbes beamed at all and sundry as Harry went to the pulpit.

"Fear not, good folk," he said. "I have not come here to harangue you, but to have you listen to a remarkable idea. I hardly need to mention that it is a brilliant idea. Therefore, not one of mine. Mary, please come and explain."

He descended and made way for Mary to ascend the steps. She, being schoolmistress, was hardly fazed by speaking in public.

"Bread," she began. And that was enough to galvanize attention. "Most of you will remember those perfect days when my mother and father supplied bread, cakes, pies, and pastries to the town. Unfortunately, Master Shooter proved a poor successor – and a rather mean-spirited one at that!"

That got a response!

"Well, how lovely would it be if those wonderful days were to return?" Mary went on. "Well, the house still stands but the bakehouse is no more. My idea is quite simple, but has, to the best of my knowledge, never been tried before. If enough good citizens were to contribute to the rebuilding of the bakehouse, then those days *could* return. It would mean that the people who contributed would be the owners of the bakehouse and the business that was carried out there. Whatever their contribution was would be returned to them by an equal percentage of the profits generated. We would in fact have a cooperative enterprise."

"Hold fast!" Came a voice from the back. "You are saying that, should I contribute five percent of the money necessary, then I would receive five percent of the profits?"

"Exactly that," Mary nodded. "That is what I meant by a cooperative enterprise. Something that is run by the town, for the benefit of the town."

That caused a buzz of conversation, some of it quite animated. Mary let it go on for a bit before calling again for their attention.

"If the idea is appealing, then we would need swift contributions, the hire of tradesmen and materials to complete the work, plus a committee chosen by you to oversee the business itself. Now – one more thing. If you should agree, then my mother and father would be willing to move back into the house to oversee the actual baking. We have two excellent apprentices to do the actual work, aided by young Charlie. They have already proved their worth. So – I have said enough. I will leave you to discuss it between yourselves for half an hour."

She stepped down and received a grin and a wink from Harry. Excited voices throughout the church voiced opinions – the hubbub was an unusual occurrence in a house of worship!

At the end of thirty minutes, Mary again mounted the steps and asked for quiet. Sam Fewings, sexton and churchwarden grabbed the initiative and stood up.

"We simply do not believe that you have proposed this plan without considering the necessary costs," he almost prompted.

Mary gave him a broad grin. "You would be correct, Sam – I have. The materials and building costs amount to seventy pounds. That includes the building itself, the new ovens, tables, troughs, implements, and the labour required. May I ask for a show of hands from those who might be tempted to contribute?"

Many hands were raised. Mary did a quick count.

"Forty-eight hands were raised. If my instant mathematics are correct, each of those would need to contribute just under one pound and ten shillings each. Does that still have the same appeal?"

Apparently, it did. There was almost a roar of approval.

"Then, I must ask those who wish to contribute to form a committee that will be in charge of the operation. I cannot take any further part as it would be improper. Thank you all for your attendance."

Mary, her part completed, stepped down and gathered Harry by the arm to walk back home. They left behind them a church alive with people almost falling over one another to further the scheme.

"You, beloved wife, are a jewel beyond price," Harry gave her a squeeze.

"It seemed to go down well," Mary admitted with a tiny sense of pride.

Sir Paul Larkin arrived back at Brimley later that same afternoon. Safe within a leather pouch was the parchment bearing the king's seal and signature. He was a knight of the realm. Never in his wildest dreams had he envisaged such an outcome in his life. He had been staunchly against the old king – had proved that with his service to parliament and its army. But now, because of a strange twist of fate and the totally unexpected find on the moor, he had earned the gratitude of a king that he thought privately to be a mere figurehead, a man bent upon his own pleasure to the exclusion of anything else.

However, he was as sensible as anyone else to the fact of his elevation – and not a trifle proud. He dismounted and handed the reins of his favourite horse to the stable boy, then strode into the house where Luke Farmer and some of the staff were waiting to welcome him home.

"Welcome home again, master," Luke grinned. "You will find everything in readiness."

"What is all this 'master' nonsense?" Larkin shouted in mock anger. "Have you no idea how to address me?"

Luke had never seen this side of the master before. Obviously, something had gone terribly awry with his visit to Westminster. Was the master in deep trouble? If so, were the household also about to suffer as a consequence?

Larkin sniffed and drew out the parchment, unrolled it and handed it to Luke.

"Read that aloud!" he commanded.

Fearing that such an important – and signed – document had been produced, Luke feared the worst. The estate was confiscated, and all were to be cast out upon the streets. And then he read the very first line.

"Be it known that His Majesty Charles by the grace of God King of England, Scotland and Ireland being most grateful for the loyal service of Sir Paul Larkin -," he read aloud, and paused.

"My humble apologies, Sir Paul. I had no idea. And please accept all of our congratulations and admiration at your elevation."

"Master steward," Larkin cast a great grin at the assembled staff. "Kindly gather every single member of the estate into the hall and ensure that the cask of finest wine is there as well. And in future, I shall expect the lowest of bows and the deepest of curtseys from every one of you!"

He ended with a great guffaw that had everyone laughing and grinning like idiots. And how would young Jamie take to being officially my squire, he wondered? That young man had been the one to find the badge. He would certainly be richly rewarded.

A letter arrived for Harry the very next morning. His usual habit was to toss letters on his desk, to be opened when he had the time. This letter seemed to demand his instant attention in that it bore the seal of the sheriff.

He could hardly believe the contents of the letter when he read it through for the first time. Upon second reading, he was equally astounded and immediately went in search of Mary.

She was, as usual, sitting at her desk in the schoolroom, writing a plan for her next lesson on the subject of mathematics – percentages, to be exact. She looked up and saw that her husband's face bore the look of someone bursting with news.

"Mary – I have just received a letter from the sheriff. He is returned from the trial and relates all that happened after we had left. It concerns the items found in that sack. The candlesticks were already returned to Lady Groombridge. Lord Templeton's box has been confiscated as he is to be summoned for trial himself. That dagger we could not identify has been rightly claimed by someone of note in Somerset. But the coins remained unclaimed. The order of the court is that, as they were discovered upon Parke land, they are to be used by the estate for whatever purpose is appropriate. Mary – there is over one hundred pounds in gold in that purse!"

"Dear merciful heavens," Mary gasped. "And, as bailiff, the determination is yours, I suppose!"

"Aye – and it presents me with the most delightful headache I have ever experienced. How on God's good earth may I arrive at a decision?"

"One thing it may *not* be used for is the new bakery," Mary stated. "There are so many people looking forward to participating in the scheme – and it is one that will be of great pride to the town. It cannot be taken from them!"

"I agree with that completely," Harry nodded. "But – what?"

"May I offer advice?" Mary asked quietly.

"Why in the name of heaven did you suppose I came her immediately if not to ask for your opinion?"

"Then, say nothing whatsoever to anyone else. Let us both put our heads together and discuss any possibility – no matter how odd they may seem. It is something that must be got absolutely right!"

"May we not broaden our thinking to include others who may have good ideas – and who can be trusted to keep silent?"

"Such as whom?" Mary enquired.

"James and Avril Ramsey – your aunt and uncle!"

"Would that not open us to a charge of nepotism?"

"No – everyone would expect that wise old pair to be consulted!"

"Reverend Forbes?"

"Aye – he would have very good ideas."

"But no more than that. We would have five brains working on the puzzle. I wonder what ideas may emerge?"

Rosie had at last managed to engineer a meeting between her and Jack's parents. Ella and Gil followed their daughter up to the smithy somewhat bemused by Rosie's silence. Jack was not there

– was away at Brimley for the day fitting a new gate that he and his father had made.

Simon saw the three coming towards the open smithy and ducked his head into a large bucket of water. He was extremely hot!

Having dried his head on a large towel, he ushered his three visitors into the parlour where Imelda was sitting darning a hole in one of Simon's tunics. Of Rachael there was no sign.

"It seems we have a delegation descended upon us," Simon grinned, making for the ale barrel.

"I have needed to speak to all of you for some days now," Rosie was determined to get to the point immediately. "Jack spoke to me last week and what he said caused me some grave concern. He seemed to believe that being close cousins formed no barrier to a relationship of a more intimate kind than is proper."

"Dear God," Simon gasped. "That lad has the brains of a dead frog. Whatever possessed him to believe that you would agree to such an arrangement?"

Imelda was not quite so vehement. "I did wonder whether some such notion was churning away inside his head. I have seen him cast eyes on Rosie more than once. Of course, had he said anything, I would have told him firmly that such an idea was illegal, immoral, and just plain wrong!"

"Oh, believe me, I told him exactly that," Rosie answered. "But rather than see the truth of my statement, he just seemed downcast – almost as if he saw that as no barrier whatsoever!"

"I have to agree with Imelda," Ella added her thoughts. "I have also wondered from his actions whether he had feelings for Rosie that were beyond the bounds of cousinly affection."

"And, as usual, I suppose that Simon and I had no notion whatsoever – being mere males and totally unobservant," Gil grunted.

"Please, whatever you do, do not punish him too severely," Rosie pleaded. "I know he is utterly misguided, but I honestly believe he saw no wrong in what he proposed. Perhaps he actually *does* have deep feelings for me. I hold no antipathy towards him and would never wish harm to come to him for his honest speech."

Simon grunted and sat his great weight on the chair that he had personal made. It was the only one that could be guaranteed not to collapse.

"I shall not beat him, skin him alive, boil his head in the trough. But – Imelda and I will talk very seriously to him when he returns. He has to rid himself of these notions. But how we may accomplish that I have no clear idea."

"Rosie, you did the right thing in telling us all about the matter," Ella regarded her daughter with some pride. She knew that Rosie had found it difficult.

"Aye – you did the only thing possible," Gil agreed.

"What we simply must do is to keep this from anyone else's ears," Imelda cautioned. "There are some hereabouts who would like nothing more than to berate him as sinful!"

"And that includes Rachael," Simon growled. "That young miss has had enough to deal with from those wretched twins!"

"You know, I honestly believe that Peterkin only went along with it for the sake of brotherly unity," Ella mused. "I know that Mary feels the same way."

"Then, in the name of the saints, why did he not stop it before it started?" Simon demanded.

"That, I cannot tell you," Ella replied. "But, not being a twin, how may any of us understand what passes between them? What tight bond of loyalty exists?"

"I cannot answer that," Simon muttered. "But I shall guard our Racheal from harm, no matter from which source it arises."

"As to the matter of Jack, rest assured that Simon and I shall take him firmly to task. Where that may lead, I have no idea," Imelda stated.

Jamie at first didn't know how to react when he learned of Larkin's knighthood. His immediate reaction was to be happy for his 'boss' but wondered where on earth that left him. Would Larkin even bother to continue with his exploration? He was not kept in suspense very long. Larkin summoned him to Brimley with the excuse that they needed to finalise their future plans. That, at least, told Jamie that there was a future for him as well.

"Now, do not dare bow when you come into the same room as I occupy," Larkin gave him a broad grin of welcome. "We are still the same people we always were. Now that you are here, I have to tell you that my knighthood came about solely because I returned that badge to the king. But – and here is the important point – I did not find it. Neither did I discover its importance. You did both of those things. Therefore, my elevation is solely down to your efforts – and I am deeply aware of that fact. In days of old, you would automatically be my squire. But as those days of knightly endeavour are well and truly past, I have to devise some other way in which you can share in the reward."

"I was simply doing my job," Jamie said, wondering where this conversation was heading.

"Yes, you were. But you went further than what anyone might have expected – your natural curiosity took over and made the discovery. I have wondered how that diligence might be rewarded – and I have come up with a solution. So, sit you down and tell me what you think of the idea."

Jamie drew out a stool and sat down opposite Larkin, wondering again what would emerge. He had never even dreamed of what he was about to hear.

"Most of this country of England is already mapped – mostly by order of past kings and governments. There are still areas which are not – and Dartmoor, Exmoor, parts of Yorkshire, Westmorland, and other very sparsely populated places. We have made a good start on Dartmoor and, by the time we have finished, we will have very valuable documents – the map itself, the book of notes and descriptions, plus the history that emerges. My plan is to form our investigations into a proper business. That business shall have two members to start with – you and me. Because I have made the financial investment, I shall retain three quarters of the business, making you the junior partner owning the other quarter. You will be free to suggest whatever you believe is the best course of action – and I shall always consult you before setting a plan into motion. Now, young man, how does that appeal to you?"

"But I am still only of seventeen summers," Jamie stuttered.

"And that mere fact precludes you from participating in this endeavour?"

"I have yet to reach my majority. In the eyes of the law, I am still a child."

"Then the law, as has been stated many times, is an ass. In three months from now, you will reach your lawful majority. As far as I am concerned, you reached it some time ago when you demonstrated your aptitude and diligence. So, do you agree?"

"Well, as you express confidence in me so readily, I agree with much gratitude. I shall do my best to earn that confidence."

"Excellent! I have drawn up a partnership contract and have signed it. You are now my junior partner – and I could not wish for a better one! Let us start work again this coming Monday and set a hard and fast plan for the next six months."

Later that day, Jamie returned home and showed the contract to his parents and to his sister. Even Rosie showered him with congratulations.

"You are indeed a son to be proud of," Gil gave his son a manly hug. Ella took her turn and gave him a motherly one. Rosie simply patted her young brother on the head and blew him a kiss.

Jamie went to bed that night with his head in a bit of a whirl.

CHAPTER XVIII

By the first week of April, Larkin and Jamie had departed for the moor to begin again where they had left off the previous early winter. The relationship between Kent and Maud Fletcher was known throughout the town. What was not known to anyone but the immediate family was the awkwardness between Jack and Rosie.

James and Avril split the visits to patients and the attention to those who called at the apothecary between themselves and Rosie. More and more, they relied upon Rosie to take responsibility for visits, diagnoses, treatment, prognoses, and general healing. Apart from anything else, it took her mind completely off other matters. She was slowly becoming a medical recluse.

Nell brought Kate for yet another visit on the second Sunday of the month. By then, Nell's pregnancy was advanced to the point that everyone immediately knew from her mere appearance.

"And what news do you bring this time?" James asked as they sat down to a late dinner.

"Merely further news of the business," Nell replied. "Adam has been trading for a month or more now. It is firmly established and is doing very well. Kate now has a new vessel named for her, do you not, sweetie?"

"It's called The Sweet Kate," the little girl looked up from her platter of beef and vegetables. "It has three sails, and the master is called Wobbly."

"Er – his actual name is Webley, and he came to us from Adam's own father. He made one journey for that horrid business and came begging to Adam for release. He and his whole crew were almost on their knees, begging to be taken from what they regarded as the devil's own work. They have served very well since they started."

"My little sister is kicking, and mama lets me feel her tummy!" Kate announced.

"I keep telling her that it may be a little brother," Nell laughed.

"But as long as you and the little one thrives it will not matter whether it be brother or sister," Avril stated, giving Kate a small frown.

Rosie looked up at that point.

"I was determined that Jamie would be a sister for me. I well remember bursting into tears when mama said it didn't matter. But after Jamie was born, I came to realise that it just *didn't* matter. I had a little one to help look after and love – and that was all that *did* matter!"

"Are you going to be a real apof-cry, Aunt Rosie?"

"Believe me, she already is," James asserted.

"But not in the eyes of the law!" Rosie pouted.

"In the eyes of all in this town you have helped to heal, you most certainly are. As has your Aunt Avril been these many years!"

"And as Nell would have been!" Avril added.

It was late that same afternoon that Harry was summoned by one of the stable hands.

"Come quick, Master Bailiff – Master Peterkin is lying outside the pigsty and bleeding. Master Ostler is tending him."

Harry shot outside, yelling for Mary and Hob to come and join him. He rushed through the big house, out the kitchen door and across the large courtyard to where he could see the ostler and a couple of other men from the gardens bending over a body that lay prostrate on the ground.

Peterkin lay huddled over, almost foetus-like, his hands clutched around his middle. Underneath his curled-up body, a pool of blood was slowly trickling towards the shallow gutter. Harry gave a bellow and knelt by the side of his son. He yelled for Mary – if anyone could be of greatest use, it was his medically trained wife.

"Hold still, son," he whispered. "Try not to move until your mother has examined you." He put one hand on Peterkin's shoulder and another on the hip so as to keep the lad still.

Mary ran across to her son. She did not scream in anguish, nor did she shed a tear. She went to Peterkin's other side and very calmly started to examine where the blood was coming from. She gently raised Peterkin's grubby shirt to expose his chest and abdomen – and there was the wound for all to see. A deep gash formed a straight line from just above the navel to just below the bottom rib on the left side.

Much to Harry's consternation, Mary stood up and went to the kitchen. She came back with a wad of clean linen and a bowl of clean water. Rinsing her fingers, she gently probed the wound and sat back on her heels with a sigh of relief.

"Tis deep but has done no really serious damage," she announced. "What we must do is to get him inside the house and lying flat so that I may cleanse the wound properly and then sew it closed. With proper care, it should heal naturally."

She turned to Hob and asked him to organise a plank for Peterkin to be laid on, then carried carefully to the dining table.

Harry started to breathe normally as his son was carried tenderly into the house. Mary then summoned the young messenger to go as fast as possible to the apothecary for poppy juice and the necessary salves. Harry thanked all who had helped and asked everyone except Mary and Hob to leave them. All obeyed except for one of the gardeners. He waited until all the others had left before approaching Harry.

"Master Bailiff, I thought it best to show you this in private," he muttered, holding out a large knife that was smeared with blood. "I discovered it at the side of the pigsty and thought it best to wait until now when you were more able to deal with it."

Harry took the proffered knife by the end of the handle, thanked the gardener, then turned to Mary when the door closed.

"Tis Will's knife," he said.

"Dear God above – what has he done?" Mary gasped.

Hob just looked at the knife and gave a sigh. "Shall I go and find him?" he asked.

"If he has any sense, he will be on his knees before the altar begging forgiveness. God may find it possible to forgive, but I am going to find it very difficult. Hob – please start a search and bring him here if you are successful."

When the messenger returned with the necessary items, Mary mixed a powerful dose of the poppy juice and started to rouse Peterkin. All the time, she had instructed Harry to keep the wad of linen pressed to the wound to help stop the bleeding.

"Wha -?" Peterkin slowly opened one eye and gazed at his mother.

"Hush – and drink this down. I am going to have to cleanse the wound and then sew it together – and that *is* going to hurt. This drink will make most of the pain go away."

"Will it make me drunk like Uncle Abel used to be?"

"No – but you will be very sleepy. With luck, you may even fall deep asleep. When you wake up, it will all be over. Now, drink up and trust in me."

Harry watched absolutely fascinated as the wound was cleansed, gently sewn together, then smeared with a special salve. Lengths of clean linen were wound around and secured in place.

"There," Mary announced, washing her hands for the fifth time. "All done and as neatly sewn as I have ever managed. He will probably sleep for some hours now, so he needs be lifted gently and taken up to his bed. I shall inspect the wound again before nightfall."

"And thank the good lord for such a competent wife and mother," Harry kissed Mary. "And now to the matter of Will. What in the name of heaven caused him to inflict such injury upon his twin brother?"

"I suspect it all goes back to that disgraceful jape upon Rachael," Mary thought aloud. "Now – where is Lauren?"

"You believe that Lauren will know the whys and wherefores?" Harry asked.

"Oh, believe me, Harry. Lauren knows the whys and wherefores of everything that happens within a five-mile radius. She is Hob reincarnated as a girl!"

"But she is always so quiet and restrained – unlike Hob who used to hare about at the speed of lightning!"

"Nevertheless, Hob knew everything that went on. As does our daughter – but far more circumspectly. When Peterkin is settled, we must search her out.

That evening saw another supper date between Kent and Maud Fletcher. This time, it happened at Maud's own house – a large cottage in the centre of the main street where she and her sister May had been brought up by their deceased mother and father.

"That, my dearest Maud, was utterly delicious," Kent declared as he finished the final course of a set egg custard with glazed sugar on the top.

"Please believe me when I say that I honestly *did* prepare it all by myself," Maud could not help but be pleased at the result of her labours.

"Probably the finest artist in silk embroidery as well as a highly accomplished cook. That is quite some combination," Kent grinned at her in admiration.

"A combination sufficient to maintain your interest in me?" Maud asked quietly.

"Without a moment's hesitation," Kent replied, equally quietly. "We are neither of us in the flush of youth. We are older and wiser and careful in our dealings with others. But one thing I have come to realise is that we are very comfortable in one another's company – and you cook divinely!"

Maud looked across the small table and fixed him with her eyes.

"And?" she prompted.

"Maud Fletcher – would you do me the great honour of becoming my wife?" he enquired gently.

"And I thought the day would never dawn," she gave him her sweetest smile. "Yes, Matthew – I would be honoured to become your wife."

Kent was, for a moment, struck dumb for words. He also had never thought the day would dawn when he would find himself a perfect partner. But in Maud, he knew that she was just that person.

"And how may we broadcast this momentous news?" Maud laughed. "After all, we shall have to have banns read and posted so it will soon become common knowledge."

"Aye – we must announce it well before that happens," Kent agreed. "We owe it to many people to ensure that they do not find out after the event, so to speak."

Maud was silent for a while.

"Matthew – would you consider us living here in this cottage? It is larger than the one you rent – and there would be no need for rent anyway. I own this house."

"And so you still shall," Kent nodded. "It is a fine idea. I shall have a special contract drawn up that ensures that your ownership of the house does not automatically become mine when we wed. That state of affairs is archaic – that a man automatically owns his wife's property. It shall not happen to us!"

"That will cause many a legal eyebrow to be raised," Maud laughed.

"It has been said many times that the law is an ass. We shall tweak its tail!"

Mary had checked twice on Peterkin before supper. He was awake and complaining that the stitches were pulling and making him very uncomfortable. Despite her best efforts, she was unable to get her son to say one word about how he had sustained the injury.

Harry, meanwhile, had sent search parties out to find Will – and all had returned empty handed. Nobody they spoke to had seen the lad. Even Hob, usually the fount of all local knowledge, declared himself stumped.

Feeling that Will would come home eventually to face the music, Mary and Harry sat down to a late supper. In one sense relieved that Peterkin would suffer no lasting damage, they nevertheless were apprehensive about Will. It was with a sense of relief that they saw Lauren come to join them at table.

Whilst the twin boys were fourteen years of age, Lauren was just ten. But both Mary and Harry knew that, should they ever want serious answers, they were far more likely to get considered answers from Lauren.

"We have both been searching for you," Mary said as Lauren helped herself to some bread, cheese and weak ale.

"Yes, mama – I know," Lauren did not even look up from her platter.

Harry, never having the patience of his schoolmistress wife, threw down his knife and favoured his daughter with a scowl.

"Do not even pretend that you do not know what has happened," he growled. "Not only do you know, but I suspect you know the reason for it. So, young madam, talk to us!"

Lauren turned large, blue eyes on her father. Then, seeing that her 'little girl' wiles would avail her nothing, gave a resigned shrug.

"Peterkin has been on and on at Will ever since they played that prank upon Rachael. Will was adamant that it was a harmless jape, but Peterkin was full of remorse for the hurt they had caused."

"Aye, we well knew all that," Harry said. "But – it then came to a head with Will taking his knife to his brother. Why?"

"This very morning, I overheard Will shout to Peterkin that he was weak and stupid to make such a fuss about a harmless prank. Peterkin replied that Will could call him all the names under heaven, and he would still regret what they had done."

"And you managed to overhear this how?" Mary asked.

"I was at the other side of the pigsty looking to the health of that little runt – the one pushed out by the others."

"And neither twin knew you were there?"

"I suppose not, mama – or they would not have been so loud in their argument."

"You have told us the words used but it is important to know how those words were delivered. Were they shouted in anger? Spoken softly?"

"Oh, both were shouting at one another. And when Peterkin said that he never would participate in another of Will's schemes, Will shouted back that he had no further use for him as a brother."

"And now tell me honestly, were you still there when Will took his knife to his brother?"

"No, mama. I feared that I would be discovered. So, I crept away. I am sure neither knew I had heard them arguing."

Mary gave her daughter a smile of thanks for her honesty.

"And as Peterkin refuses to say how the attack happened, all we can do is to wait for Will's return," Harry grunted.

"Papa – what if Will is so scared that he does *not* return?" Lauren gave voice to what Mary feared.

"And where might he go? He is but fourteen years of age and is very well known hereabouts. The fact of his action will already be known for miles around – no secret is safe in Bovey! He will hardly find a safe place to hide!"

"He said some weeks past that he wished to walk to Plymouth and take work aboard ship. He saw no future for himself here; he said that he was bored to distraction and needed adventure."

"And how is it that you have only just revealed that to us?" Harry demanded.

"Because I was not meant to overhear what he said – and I feared you and mama would be cross with me for listening into what was not my business."

"Oh, Lauren – cannot you see that it *was* your business? You are a part of this family, as are Will and Peterkin. The whole family needed to know!" Mary spoke quietly to her daughter.

"So, now we know that he definitely *has* some plan in mind. It is far too close now to nightfall. But on the morrow, I shall raise as many mounted as I can muster so that we may cover every road towards Plymouth. There is little any of us can do before then," Harry immediately started listing mentally who would be needed. Those two trackers for a start.

"Pray heaven that he is found before he can commit to something so dangerous," Mary almost folded her hands in prayer.

Neither Harry nor Mary slept much that night. Harry, because he was planning; and Mary because she kept watch over Peterkin. It was well after midnight when Lauren came to join her. Mother and daughter sat side by side for the rest of the night. Mary knew that her son would recover but felt that her only place was by his bedside.

Peterkin woke up as the cockerel started his morning fanfare. That was echoed in the distance by the three cockerels owned by Gil and Ella.

Peterkin winced a bit as he sat up in bed, then noted that his mother and sister were sitting in the window seat.

"Er, good morning. I'm very hungry," he managed.

"First things first," Mary said, going to the bedside. "First, I examine the wound and apply more salve and a new dressing. And then, if I deem it right, you may rise and come downstairs to break your fast.

Lauren watched fascinated as her mother expertly re-dressed the wound.

"No weeping of blood, so my stitches have worked their magic. Right, my son, up with you and do everything very carefully. Neither you nor I want to have to repair broken stitches!"

"Has Will come back?" Peterkin asked.

"No, he has not. And your father is already summoning people necessary to search for him on his way to Plymouth. Yes – you need not look so startled – we *do* know about his foolhardy plan!"

"But I would never have said a word about it!" Peterkin said. "Lauren – did you tell them?"

"Yes, I did," Lauren replied, very firmly. "They needed to know as it is a stupid plan and would have deprived me of a brother and you of a twin!"

"Our mother and father will thank you; I can forgive you; but Will never shall!"

"Then I shall have to live with his hatred. But I know it was the right thing to do."

"Indeed, it was," Mary gave her daughter a hug.

Rachael sat over her breakfast and looked disconsolately at her brother Jack.

"Is it right, what everyone is saying, that Will stabbed Peterkin and then ran away?"

"That is what everyone is saying," Jack nodded, then added, "and the bailiff is gathering parties to search for him. I hope they find him and bring him back to face his punishment!"

"Is all of this because of that damnable letter?" Rachael asked.

"Probably," Imogen answered her daughter. "It seems from all I hear that Peterkin was far more remorseful than Will. Perhaps it all boiled over into an argument that Will ended with his knife."

"This wretched matter needs to be ended," Simon grunted. "Poor Billy is being ragged unmercifully, Rachael has been humiliated, and now it seems that Peterkin has paid a sad price."

"Shall I go and speak with Peterkin and say I forgive him his part? It seems that he is at least sorry for all the hurt it has caused. I would not wish him to suffer more than he already has."

Simon and Imogen regarded their daughter with tenderness.

"That would be a very merciful act," Simon agreed. "As you say, he has already paid a heavy price."

"Then I shall visit and first tell Miss Mary what I intend."

Almost at first light, Harry had gathered three search parties. He would lead one of them with two of the estate workers. He would take a 'northern' route through Ashburton and onwards. Hob led a second team towards Totnes and then south. Sam Garvey and Robert Hook would set out alone on the 'southern' track – through Newton Abbot, then through Shipley and onwards to the west. Each party would go no further than they would be able to return before nightfall. Each went 'armed' with packs of food and flasks of ale. By eight o'clock, all had set out on their routes.

During the briefing, Harry had reminded everyone that Will had left Parke no earlier than two o'clock the previous afternoon. He therefor would have had a maximum of six hours of daylight. Nobody believed for one moment that the lad, all on his own, would travel after nightfall. He was definitely on foot – therefore, could have travelled no more than twenty miles. It would take the mounted searchers just two hours to reach his overnight stop if they kept up a steady canter.

By eleven o'clock, Harry and his two had passed through Ashburton and Buckfastleigh – and had seen no sign of Will. Hob was nearing Totnes, having gone through Ipplepen and Littlehempston. They also had not found any trace of the lad. Garvey and Hook had taken a more southerly route and were just about level with the track that led down to Berry Pomeroy and its ruined castle. They would have to go slightly north to Totnes as there was no other way to cross the Dart unless they went all the way south and took a ferry across to Dartmouth – and that seemed to them to be futile. So, they headed along a well-used road towards the town of Totnes.

It was just about the time when most folk in Bovey Tracey were stopping work for their midday dinner when two very large carts arrived and came to rest at the vacant cottage next to the school. There were two men on each cart, one driving and one ready to assist in unloading. A rather florid man and an equally florid woman rode horses behind the carts. Their arrival caused little or no interest because most people were indoors.

The large carts were unloaded of furniture, bedding, clothes, chests of various sizes. The woman supervised where each was to be put, then dismissed the two carts and their personnel with a haughty wave. She disappeared inside the cottage as a smaller cart arrived. On it were smaller items, plus two small servant girls. These were quickly put to work.

The large man, flamboyantly dressed in scarlet breeches, white, ruffled shirt, and emerald green coat, emerged and placed a tall, feathered hat on his head. He strode purposefully down towards the mill, using a silver topped cane. He stopped at the apothecary's and strode to the door. He pushed it wide open and announced his presence with a bellow of, 'Ho within!'

Avril, who was on 'shop' duty that day, came bustling through, wiping her lips on a napkin as she was just half-way through her dinner. She surveyed the large man, not recognising him as from anywhere local.

"Yes – may I help you?" she enquired politely.

"I sincerely doubt that," came a gravel-voiced reply. "I am Doctor Elbert Eustace and am now this town's medicus. You will cease immediately seeing patients. You will cease prescribing your potions. I shall prescribe what is to be administered – and you will supply what I order. I hope I make myself perfectly clear!"

Avril was at first taken aback by the abrupt and unmannerly address. But then her hackles started to rise.

"And what if the good people of this town – people we have known all our lives and who trust us – simply refuse to be browbeaten in such a manner?" she asked.

"I intend to make it abundantly clear that I am the qualified doctor and that seeking advice from country quacks such as yourselves is to stop immediately."

"And you will no doubt charge handsomely for all this service?"

"Naturally! My training and expertise are worth the coin that I charge. There shall be no more free medicine in this town!"

James and Rosie came through, having witnessed the loud voice of the doctor.

"And what of the poor people down on the Heath?" James asked quietly. "Shall they be doomed to perish for lack of money?"

"It is like I said," Eustace boomed. "If they cannot pay, then they must borrow!"

"If you believe for one moment that the people of this town will meekly succumb to your extortion, then you have a lot to learn," James retorted. "We have seen them through thick and thin, winters of fever, outbreaks of disease. They will not abandon us for the sake of enriching you!"

"Can he do as he threatens?" Rosie asked, as the man stumped off up the street.

"He can try – and I guarantee he shall not succeed!" Avril gave Rosie a reassuring grin.

Rosie went to work that afternoon in a very uneasy frame of mind. Her whole life was bound up with the apothecary business. Without it, she would be utterly lost.

Garvey and Hook were at the top of the hill that would take them down to the bridge that spanned the Dart, and which would then take them the short distance into Totnes.

"Look," Hook pointed at a lone figure trudging down the hill about a quarter of a mile in front of them. "Do you reckon that could be young Will?"

"Could be, I suppose," Garvey squinted his eyes trying to make out the build of the figure.

Garvey went to the left of the road whilst Hook went to the right. On the thick grass, their hoofbeats would be muffled as they allowed their mounts to trot towards the figure.

By the time they were less that one hundred yards from what they now could see was a youngish fellow, there was no disguising the noise of the horses. The young man glanced behind him, and suddenly took off to the right and into the trees.

"Now that's just plain stupid!" Garvey grunted. He crossed the road and made a grab for the reins of Hook's horse as Hook himself slid out of the saddle and went haring after the fellow – who they had both recognised as young Will.

Hook simply followed a trail of flattened grass and broken twigs. It was not the hardest track he had ever had to follow. Some distance into the wood, he halted as the sounds in front of him had stopped. Hook gave a grin and walked silently forward until he was standing under the branches of an ash tree.

"Will – do not be an idiot. I know that you are up there. Come down and we'll get this mess sorted out."

Garvey had followed, leading the two horses. He stopped and gave a smile, pointing upwards. Hook simply nodded.

"Look, Will," Garvey said quietly. "We are charged with bringing you back to Master Bailiff. Hob and a couple of others are doing the same, as is Master Bailiff himself. We can either wait for you to come down, or one of us will simply come up and get you."

From above came the sound of a quiet sob. Garvey and Hook simply stood under the tree and said nothing.

"I really did not mean to hurt him," came from above between gulps. "He just would not stop berating me!"

"The first thing you need to know is that young Peterkin is not badly injured," Hook called up. "You did not stab him – your blade simply sliced him open a bit. Your own mother attended to his wound and sewed it up so that it will heal, given time."

"You swear he is not dead?"

"Aye – we both swear that he is sitting up at home, bandaged up and slowly healing."

After a few minutes, Will slowly descended and landed on the ground. Garvey and Hook made no move towards him.

"Right – what we now have to do is to get you back home. Probably the best option is for you to come with us into Totnes. Hob will probably be there with your father later today. And then we can get you a lift."

Will stayed very quiet on the short walk down into Totnes where, later that afternoon, they all met up. What Will said to his father was kept well away from everyone else, but it was noticeable that Will was mounted as pillion behind one of the grooms for the return journey.

The reunion between the twins was muted, neither wanting to say much in front of everyone else.

"What we shall now do is to get you both to bed. We shall meet here in the parlour tomorrow after we have eaten and then discuss what happened and what we shall decide for the future." Harry was quite neutral in his expression. He needed to have a long talk with Mary.

CHAPTER XIX

Will had spent the night on a pallet in the last of the spare rooms in the cottage. Needless to say, he had not slept well. Peterkin on the other hand, had spent a peaceful night of deep sleep in his own bed. He woke up realising that his wound had started to itch – and regarded this as a very positive sign.

Harry and Mary had talked well into the night, wondering how things might be brought back to an even keel. It was past midnight when they finally agreed upon a course of action – then fell asleep.

The first thing that Mary did was to examine, cleanse, then re-bind the wound.

"That is healing very nicely," she sat back quite satisfied with her work.

"It is itching," Peterkin groused. "But you always say this is a good thing."

"Indeed, it most certainly is," Mary agreed. "Now – get dressed and come downstairs. We all need to have a good talk. But first, eat and drink."

Breaking the fast was a very subdued affair that ended with Harry announcing that the family would not be disturbed for the next hour – no matter what emergency arose. Hob would deal with anything untoward.

"Please may I speak first, papa?" Will quavered.

Harry glanced at Mary, then nodded.

"I must first apologise to Peterkin," Will began his prepared speech. "I am truly sorry that I wounded you and wish only that I could go back so that I might control my temper with you."

"You tried to stab me," Peterkin regarded his brother with a look of sorrow rather than one of anger. "If I had not turned aside, I might now be very seriously wounded – or dead!"

"I am really truly sorry," Will mumbled.

"But all I was trying to do was to make you realise that what we did with that letter was wrong and hurtful," Peterkin pointed out.

Harry had been drumming his fingers on the table as he listened to the twins. He looked up and faced Will.

"Your mother and I believe you when you say that you are truly sorry for the injury you inflicted upon Peterkin. But let us go back to the cause of the matter – the letter. Do you have any regrets that you caused it to be sent to Rachael?"

"No, not really," Will looked defiant. "To my mind, it was simply a jape."

"Then, let me put a different case to you. Let us suppose that someone had sent a similar letter to your sister Lauren. What would be your thoughts then?"

Will sat for a moment before replying – still with a defiant look on his face.

"I would have expected Lauren to take it as a harmful jest," he stated very firmly. "But Lauren is still far too young to receive such a letter!"

Both Mary and Harry regarded Will with some consternation.

"You really do *not* see what harm and hurt you have done, do you?" Harry said.

"We play jests upon one another all the time," Will retorted. "Peterkin put a dead mouse in my boots; I spread salt on Lauren's porridge; Charlie from the dairy put worms into a pie from the bakery. They are just jests!"

"Yes, those *are* just jests," Mary agreed. "But that letter preyed upon peoples' feelings, causing dismay and hurt. It made a laughingstock of poor Billy and reduced Rachael to tears. That, Will, was most certainly *not* a jest. And if you are unable to see the difference then there is something inherently cruel in your nature. And I for one cannot fathom where you developed such cruelty."

"It was just a bit of fun!" Will shouted.

"No, it was not!" Harry shouted back. "It was an act of cruelty."

"You should not have stopped me going to Plymouth. I would then no longer have been a thorn in your side," Will muttered.

"Are you that determined to leave this family?" Harry asked.

"As you are ashamed of me, then the sooner I am gone, the better for all concerned!" Will yelled at his father.

Harry went very quiet, as did Mary. Will sat and glowered, whilst Peterkin sat and looked aghast.

"It would seem," Harry started again slowly and deliberately, "that no manner of physical punishment would alter you; neither would another three months at some menial task. As you are determined to carry on as if you have done no wrong, it would be better that you went somewhere where you may learn discipline the hard way. I shall speak to the sheriff and have you enrolled as one of his trainee soldiers. Believe me, that gives me no pleasure whatsoever. You have caused hurt and shame to our friends; you have injured your brother. Enough is enough!"

"I shall learn to be a proper fighting man, not some puny lad, fit only to muck out pigs!" Will came back at him.

"It is just possible that you will learn some discipline – and how to discipline yourself. Try one of those so-called japes on your sergeant and you will *really* learn the hard way! Now, go to your room and pack whatever you may need. I shall ride with you to Exeter as soon as you are ready."

"Will – please do not do this," Peterkin pleaded with his brother. "Just acknowledge your fault and all will be well again."

"You may stay here and be a good boy," Will sneered. "I shall become a soldier and have many adventures whilst you stay here and learn your books. I cannot wait!"

"Have you no word for me?" Mary asked. "You are my first-born, my own first child. You will have my love wherever you may be. I shall never understand what is going on in your mind, but my love for you will always be there."

"You would do better to forget me, mother. I am obviously an embarrassment!"

Will stood up and marched out of the parlour. His footsteps clumped up the stairs. Mary sat with tears rolling down her face, all her years of knowledge and teaching useless in the face of such hurt. Harry sat beside her and held her close. Peterkin sat and looked as if his world had suddenly come to a stop.

Many people that morning found some excuse to visit the apothecary. Word had quickly spread that a qualified physician had come to the town to open a practice. Word had spread just as fast that he was arrogant and that his charges would be far in excess of those made by James, Avril and Rosie.

Gil, Ella and Jamie were the first to arrive. "Did he really say that his knowledge is superior to yours?" Ella asked.

"Yes, and it may well be that his book-learning is in advance of ours. But his manner will certainly earn him no friends!" James grunted.

"I doubt that many will be enticed away from your doorstep," Gil stated. "This town has a very long memory. The care and help you have given for many a year will not be forgotten in a hurry."

"I am sure that Sir Paul and those at Brimley shall not abandon you," Jamie added.

Next to arrive were Gaston, Glory and Isobel Bessant from the bookshop. They said very much the same thing.

Simon, Imogen and Rachael burst through the doors. Simon was a lot more forceful in his choice of words.

By dinner, nearly everyone in the village had found their way there – and those who could not, asked their neighbours to convey their feelings on the subject.

"It would seem that our Doctor Eustace is going to have a lean time here," James observed, wiping his platter with a hunk of bread.

Luke Barton, steward of the Parke estate, was not in the best of tempers as he arrived at the apothecary the next morning. At sixty-six years of age, and well past the normal age of retirement, he had been looking forward to his last few months in peace and quiet before handing over to his successor – who had yet to arrive.

"And what brings that mournful face into our shop?" Avril had known the steward all of her life. At fifty-three years of age, she and James were also looking forward to a life of relative peace and quiet.

"That bloody man, Eustace, has lodged a complaint against you and James. Not only lodged with me as steward, but also threatening to take the matter to a court of law."

"And what may we have done to incur his displeasure – apart from defending our record of achievement?" Avril asked.

"According to him, you have maligned him and have spoken to his detriment to his prospective patients. In other words, he is about to pursue a case of slander."

Avril did not even blink at those words.

"In point of fact, he was the one doing the maligning – ranting on about his superior knowledge and qualifications, denigrating our efforts. James and Rosie were also witnesses to the tirade he made against this business."

"I am hardly deaf and blind to the goings on," Barton grunted. "I have already heard from many sources that the people of Bovey will stay fast to you – despite his qualifications penned on parchment!"

"I was a witness, as Avril has already told you," James appeared from the parlour. He was followed by Rosie.

"What that pompous man said was deliberately provocative," Rosie remarked. "He seemed to arrive here in a mood for a fight, never once ascertaining whether his remarks had merit."

"That is certainly true," Avril agreed. "He immediately set out to belittle us, to point to his doctorate as if that was the only thing that mattered. He will soon find out that the people here will not be browbeaten!"

"I would imagine that his bedside manner will be akin to that of an offensive warthog," James laughed. "And that, plus his demand for exorbitant fees, will hardly endear him to anyone."

"I am willing to wager a considerable sum that his first recourse will involve his fleam – to take blood from the patient, no matter the symptoms!" Avril snorted.

"That will make him no better than that drunken oaf in Newton," Barton exclaimed. "Perhaps we should let him loose on a rich patient and see what transpires!"

"We would all be loath to allow that," James shook his head. "Taking blood unnecessarily can often do more harm than good."

"But I was the person who arranged his lease to the cottage," Barton looked downcast. "I just wish that I had waited until his character emerged before agreeing. I shall immediately write to Sir John, appraising him of the position. After all, his will be the final word.”

Sir John Vickery, owner of the Parke estate – and that included Bovey Tracey – spent nearly his entire life at Westminster. It would be at least five days before an answer came back.

“In the meantime, we shall endeavour to ignore the wretched doctor and carry on as normal,” James decided. “I have little doubt that the rest of the town shall do the same.”

Just before the time for midday dinner, Harry arrived back. He immediately went into the house to find Mary who would be home from school for her meal. Peterkin was mooching about, looking for all the world as if his life was close to its end.

“Sir Thomas heard me out in private,” he reported as he sat down to his dinner. “At first, he was reluctant to admit Will as a trainee when he learned of his actions and, probably more to the point, his attitude. However, I managed to persuade him to accept Will when I told him of Will’s determination to become a soldier.”

“So, Will is now in Exeter learning the ways of the army,” Mary said, a tear never far from the surface whenever she thought about her son.

“Sir Thomas enrolled him in my presence and handed him over to a sergeant who is in charge of the basic training. From the look of the man, Will is in very strong hands now. I just hope that what I have done turns out to be the right thing. For the life of me, I can think of no other!”

“Shall I ever see him again?” Peterkin was also close to tears.

Harry decided that he needed to put the best possible face on the matter.

“I can almost guarantee that you shall,” he stated as firmly as he could. “When he has been trained enough to be classed a proper soldier, he will come back here all a-swagger with his accomplishment. He will want to show that he has succeeded, that he was right in his attitude all along.”

"But he was *not* right!" Peterkin almost shouted. "All he had to do was to swallow his pride and admit fault. but no, not Will! He has to be right about everything all the time!"

Lauren, who had been sitting quietly eating her dinner, suddenly spoke up.

"Will was making advances to Rachael long before the thought of that prank," she said.

Mary looked aghast at her daughter.

"And you tell us only now?" she gasped. "Had we known of it, we would have been able to put a stop to it long before the matter degenerated into hurt and viciousness."

"You may not leave it at that," Harry demanded. "Tell us everything that you know."

"All I know is that Will made an advance to Rachael, and she told him that she was not interested, and not to bother her again."

"And how do you happen to know all that?" Harry demanded.

"Because he told me," Lauren admitted. "He also said that he would make her regret it."

"And you kept this a secret all this time when you could have told us and we could have perhaps taken steps to avoid what followed? In the name of heaven Lauren, why?" Mary glared at her daughter.

"Because he told me all this in confidence – and made me swear an oath not to reveal it," Lauren replied calmly. "But now that he is no longer here, I suppose that oath does not hold any longer."

"Did you know of this?" Harry asked Peterkin.

"No, father – I had no knowledge that Will had been spurned by Rachael. Had I known, I would never have agreed to partake in that cruel jest!"

"And Rachael would never have disclosed it because she would have wanted the whole nasty incident to go away – and who could blame her?" Mary stated.

Harry regarded Lauren for some minutes before coming to a decision.

"I cannot fault you for keeping to a sworn oath," he said quietly. "But, in future, I sincerely hope that you will think long and hard before doing so again. Do you now believe that you did wrong by taking that oath?"

"Yes, father. It was wrong and I should never have done so. But you and mama have always told us that one of the most important things in life is to keep your word – and that is what I did. But I know that I should never have given my word in the first place."

Mary had been thinking deeply.

"Tell me, Lauren," she was almost afraid to ask the question. "Having heard what Will told you, what do you believe would have been his reaction had you *not* given your word?"

"Oh, that is simple to answer, mama. Will told me that, should I not swear the oath, he would make my life a living hell!"

And that was exactly what Mary had feared. Peterkin went to his sister and put an arm about her shoulders. "You could have told me," he said.

"No, I could not. I gave my word!"

Mary gave a sigh and faced Harry.

"I was appalled when you said that Will would be taken to Exeter to learn soldiering. But in view of what has just emerged, I now acknowledge that it was definitely the correct course of action. All I can now hope is that Will emerges from all this with an improved sense of honour. But I shall never understand how any son of ours could have done what he did, and never had the sense to realise that it was wrong and shameful!"

"In some manner, we have all been deeply hurt," Harry said very quietly. "Pray that the time may come when that hurt goes away!"

Doctor Elbert Eustace set out that afternoon with the firm intention of gathering as many patients as he could. On the front door of the cottage, he had hung a wooden plaque on which in gold lettering was printed 'Doctor E Eustace MD (Oxon)'. His wife, a rather mousy woman, made a show of polishing it morning and evening.

Had he taken the time to get to know the people of the town, he would never have made a start at the very top opposite the church. John and Evelyn Ramsey had taken to their new, temporary role with gusto. Already, the new bakehouse was arising from the ashes. Mary had said that she intended to have a large sign painted when the bakehouse was complete. Phoenix Bakery, it would proclaim.

Eustace arrived full of vim and vigour. He made himself known to John and Evelyn and then started off on completely the wrong foot.

"Up until now," he boomed in his pompous tones, "this small town has had to suffer the ministrations of a pair of unqualified upstarts masquerading as apothecaries. Well, now things are to change for the better. I am here, a qualified and highly experienced doctor. I may take it that I may enrol you as patients?"

John was hardly able to keep a straight face. Evelyn simply had to turn her back.

"You are saying that James Ramsey is little better than an unqualified quack, are you?"

"Indeed, I am," Eustace replied. "And this has to stop."

"I have personally known James and Avril Ramsey for many years. They have rendered excellent service to this town and have saved many a life," John said, goading Eustace into further indiscretions.

"Probably more by luck than judgement," Eustace snorted.

"Oh, I hardly think luck enters into it, do you, Evelyn?"

Evelyn composed herself and faced forward again.

"I would say that their knowledge and skill had much more to do with it," she stated.

"Pah! Such untrained peasants should not be allowed to treat patients at all!"

"So, James in your opinion, is an untrained peasant, is he?" John asked mildly.

"He most certainly is!" Eustace almost stamped his foot.

"Then, I have to tell you something else about him," John grinned. "He is my brother, and a more dedicated person I have yet to meet. So, Doctor Bloody Eustace, I advise you to keep such slanderous thoughts to yourself. You may find others in this town far less tolerant that I am."

"I am hardly known for my tolerance," came another voice. Simon had heard the interchange between John and Eustace from the open doors of his smithy, not many yards distant from the bakery.

Eustace made as if to glare at yet another of the inhabitants he liked to believe were little more than peasants. His eye lighted upon a massive man holding an equally massive club hammer.

"You know," Simon began, almost conversationally, "people like you arrive in a small Devon town and immediately come to the conclusion that the inhabitants are of little account – ready to be browbeaten by those waving paper qualifications under our noses. So, let me put you straight – if John has not already done so. We are not impressed! What we are is insulted – and I do not take kindly to insults. So, what I have to say to you is best put into two words – bugger off! Upset any more of the people of Bovey and you may find yourself upended in the horse trough."

"You will come to regret that attitude when illness strikes," Eustace summoned his courage to attempt the last word.

"Oh, when illness strikes – as it has done many times, James, Avril and Rosie will tend to us with love and care as they have done so often in the past," Evelyn faced the doctor. "And I, as a supposed lady, cannot better Simon's advice. Bugger off!"

John stared open-mouthed at his wife of many years. He had never heard her utter words like that before.

CHAPTER XX

It was approaching the end of April when Larkin and Jamie returned from their first moor expedition of the year. As planned, they would spend a whole week cataloguing, mapping and writing up notes.

Jamie's first port of call was to his parents. They immediately bombarded him with questions – what treasures had they unearthed this time?

"None worth the mention," Jamie replied. "But that does not mean that we have not found items of great interest. Far from it. We have discovered many iron implements – or what remains of them after so many years. We have also found a few more bronze artifacts that we need to clean and study."

"Artifacts!" Rosie had seen her brother arrive and had come to welcome him home again. "My little brother now speaks of artifacts! One year past and he would not have known a bronze brooch from a loaf of bread. I doubt he would have known the meaning of the word!"

"And a very good day to you, sister!" Jamie grinned at Rosie to show that he took no offence.

"And how fares our new knight of the realm?" Ella asked.

"Oh, he is as dedicated to the search as am I," Jamie assured her. "Despite my sister's comments, I am thoroughly immersed in the business. I would never have thought that I would be, but I am."

"And are we to be allowed to view these priceless finds?" Gil enquired.

"Oh yes – that is the other piece of news that I have. Paul is setting aside one large room at Brimley for the finds to be displayed. Each will bear a card saying what it is, how old, and where it was found. In essence, it will be a small museum and I am to be its curator."

"Ye gods," Rosie pretended to swoon. "Jamie Ramsey, well-known hooligan, is growing up at long last!"

Jamie was not in the least put out. "That is something that I can agree. It *is* about time," he admitted.

Jamie stayed for dinner, then went back to Brimley to make a start on cleaning the bits and pieces they had found. He and Paul Larkin were fascinated by two of the bronze pieces – both small bowls. Washing had revealed an intricate pattern on the sides, and they were determined to discover what, if anything these patterns symbolised.

It was during the morning service the following Sunday that Reverend Forbes made the announcement of the banns for Matthew Kent and Maud Fletcher. It came as no surprise to most of the congregation as the fact of their betrothal had been common knowledge almost an hour after the proposal had been made and accepted.

There was no way the people of Bovey were going to let the announcement pass without some celebration. The two were almost frogmarched to the tavern where ale, mead and wine was drunk to their health and happiness.

"And when will the marriage take place?" Dick Allen asked on behalf of all in the tavern.

"We plan to hold the service on the third Saturday in May," Kent answered. "Everyone is invited, of course – but my purse will not stretch to a wedding feast for the whole town!"

"We shall do as we always do," Imelda chimed in. "We shall all provide a dish of some sort. All you have need to do is to pay for the ale when we drink the toast."

May was almost as happy as her sister Maud. For some years, she had wondered what would happen to her sister as she had shown no sign of being in a mood to marry anyone at all!

"See," Hob whispered to May. "She has found happiness as I told you she would!"

"You never said anything of the kind," May objected. "You were always saying that Maud was fiercely independent and would remain unwed!"

"Shall we be bridesmaids?" Kitty and Poppy were almost as excited as their mother.

"And who else but her nieces would she ask?" May replied.

"Aye – and your mother and I shall be as proud as peacocks to see to in your dresses," Hob hugged his daughters.

"I wonder what colour she shall choose?" Poppy was a bit concerned. "Pink does not suit me at all. It makes me look quite pale and ill. I hope it shall be blue as that matches my eyes."

"But it does not match mine!" Kitty, older than her sister. "I favour green!"

"It is up to your aunt Maud to choose – and whatever the choice, you shall stay quiet and agree!" May ordered.

"Yes, mama," the two muttered.

It was the same afternoon when Harry called the first meeting of his group that would decide the destination of the contents of the large purse of money. Mary had also suggested that Matthew Kent be enrolled as he and she had worked so well together when executing the will of Lady Violette. The meeting was held in the hall of Parke House. Sitting around the table were Harry, Mary, James, Avril, James Forbes, and Matthew Kent. Harry opened the meeting with a small speech of explanation.

"You will all be aware of the sack that young Bernie discovered, and what its contents were. The only item that cannot be traced and verified is the purse of coins. That purse has been awarded to us here to spend on whatever good cause or causes that we may determine. The purse contains one hundred and seven pounds in gold coinage."

Mary, who knew already, was the only one apart from Harry who failed to gasp at the mention of such a huge sum of money.

"The first thought was to place the money somewhere safe so that it could fund bursaries for children whose parents were unable to afford the small school fees. But as Matthew and I both know, that has been more than taken care of by the legacy of dear Violette."

"One problem rears its head immediately," Forbes spoke up. "As we have no idea who really owns the money, we also can have no idea what would be that person's desires. Are we therefore, starting from scratch?"

"Indeed, we are, Reverend," Harry answered. "And that is why we have gathered as many brains as possible so that every useful idea may be discussed."

"One thought occurs, one that prompted James and me to discuss the very matter this morning," Avril set the ball rolling. "We now have the very dubious pleasure of Doctor Eustace peddling his practice in the town. Some souls may just be tempted to call upon his services. But as James and I both know, his fees are exorbitant. I refrain on commenting upon the possible efficacy of his treatments! Those people who *are* tempted, could well find themselves in deep financial trouble."

"But that would mean that we were in a sense funding a man in whom we have no faith!" James argued.

"Yes, I totally agree," Avril acknowledged. "But we surely have some responsibility towards anyone who is beguiled to spend money they do not have."

"I doubt that, when put to a vote, that plan would be passed – precisely because of the wretched individual who would most benefit from our support," James was wholly against that as a plan.

Avril gave in with good grace. "But I simply had to mention it," she said quietly. "I really fear the damage that this man will do."

"Perhaps we should put a small amount by for when someone takes him to court for misdiagnosis or ill-treatment. That *would* be of benefit to the patient," Mary offered.

"What does this town most urgently need, apart from a bakery which is already being taken care of?" Harry steered the meeting back on course.

Reverend Forbes raised a hand. "In the old days, people would have come to my predecessor to confess their sins and receive absolution. Now, they come to me with all their cares, worries and tribulations. Some even come to have a private moan! There are two matters that often arise from these conversations. The first is the lack of stabling. Dick and Sal have the only one available for visiting travellers – and it simply is not big enough any longer. The second concerns the lack of sufficient access to drinking water. I am sure that both James and Avril will agree that far too many upset stomachs result from people taking river water from the most inappropriate places."

"That is absolutely true," James nodded. "But how feasible is it to locate a source that could be harnessed for common, and safe, usage?"

Kent spoke up for the first time.

"The one person who could best answer that is a military man. Wherever they go, the army has need for drinking water – for themselves and their horses. Surely, we can prevail upon someone with enough knowledge to advise us. The one person who springs immediately to mind is our new knight – Paul Larkin. He was a senior military commander and must have some idea how it may be achieved."

"I happen to know that he and Jamie are back here from the moor. Would you agree that I approach him?" Mary proposed.

"That would indeed be a good start," Harry nodded to his wife. "Now – stabling. What would be the adverse effect on Dick's and Sal's business if common stabling were to be erected and manned?"

"I can assure you that both Dick and Sal would be heartily glad to relinquish that part of their business," Forbes replied. "It is a constant headache having to tell traveller guests that their own stables were full to bursting. In fact, I would believe it to be a boon. No more turning away guests for lack of care for the horses. Their ostler and his lad would be ideal to manage the new stables but would need to recruit at least one extra helper."

"The fund of money would be needed only to erect the new stables – and I have a good idea where it may be located. Thereafter, the charges made for stabling would cover the running costs," Harry was making notes.

"Then, with stables and a water source, we have done as much as we probably can for this first meeting," Mary said. Ever the practical one, she thought it best that they concentrate on two real possibilities rather than cast about for others that might be no more than pipe dreams.

It was a further three days before an answer came from Vickery. Luke Barton's face was transformed from its usual dour expression to one of quiet satisfaction as he read the letter. He first called Grace, then Harry. All three trooped down to the apothecary to relate the news to the two most affected.

"That is a better face," Avril grinned at the Parke steward as he entered the shop. "The last time you were here, your face resembled that of a man who has just swallowed a small slug."

"Indeed, I am in a much better mood this day," Luke answered. "Let me read you a letter from his lordship." He took out the letter, unrolled it and held it at full arm's length to satisfy his lengthening eyesight. "Master Steward," he started. "I received your letter and the contents gave me a great deal of displeasure. Master James and Mistress Avril have served my manor faithfully and well for many a year and I shall not tolerate any who speak against them. Many are those in my demesne who have cause to bless them for their knowledge and careful ministration. I have instituted an enquiry into this Doctor Eustace. There is no doubt that he did qualify at the University of Oxford. He went on to open a practice in Ledbury. He was lucky to escape prosecution for malpractice and misdiagnoses – and I use the plural deliberately! His next practice opened some years later in Guildford. He was not well received there either. And now he has infested Bovey Tracey. That I shall also not tolerate. Use whatever means at your disposal to evict him from the tenancy. If necessary, tell him that I want him gone forthwith! Also, ensure that he is unable either to obtain another tenancy or to purchase a vacant property. Tell any prospective vendor that he or she shall incur my wrath should they agree to sell to him. I know that you will faithfully carry out these instructions. My regards, Vickery."

"Well," Avril gasped. "That is fairly conclusive, is it not? James and I shall write to him thanking him for his kind words and support."

"And I shall now call upon the damnable Eustace and issue his marching orders," Barton grinned.

"Much as would like to witness that, we had better keep our distance. It would seem as if we were wallowing in victory!" James laughed.

"But I, as bailiff, feel no such restraint!" Harry guffawed. "Come Master Steward – to battle!"

Those few people who were passing up and down the street paused to see the steward and bailiff knock on the large cottage door. They paused even longer when Eustace opened it and Barton began upon his speech – delivered quite deliberately at high volume.

"Doctor Eustace, I have today received firm instruction from Sir John Vickery that you are immediately to vacate the cottage. Your tenancy is terminated as of this moment. You have one hour to pack your belongings, arrange transport, and leave this town by noon this very day."

"I have a signed contract as tenant," Eustace shouted back. "Make no doubt that I shall sue through the courts for breach of that contract!"

"Then I am sure that the citizens of both Ledbury and Guildford may be prevailed upon to add their voices against you," Barton answered. "Make no mistake – should you ignore this eviction notice Master Bailiff here will ensure that it is fulfilled to the letter."

"And that I shall surely do!" Harry added.

"Good day," Luke Barton had the last word, turned on his heel and walked back to Parke. It was not until he and Grace had passed the crossroads that he permitted himself a guffaw of laughter.

CHAPTER XXI

Mary, never happier than when she was storing additional knowledge, seized the first available opportunity to visit Brimley. She was eager to see the beginnings of the new museum -and thrilled that her nephew was to be its first curator. How young Jamie had turned from the scamp of his youth into a man of learning was both a mystery and a miracle to her thinking. In that, she was not alone. Her brother Gil and sister-in-law, parents of Jamie, were also mystified. Rosie, his sister, was still not totally convinced!

Larkin was delighted to receive a visit from someone he had always admired for her energy and thirst for knowledge.

"Please, do not utter any apology," he said, ushering her into the large room. "Jamie and I are delighted that you evince such an interest."

"Hello, Aunt Mary," Jamie looked up from a huge map that he was busy filling in. "Have you come to see what we have found?"

"Wild horses could not have kept me away," Mary laughed as her eyes took in the notebooks, maps, the careful arrangement of the artifacts, and their small cards of explanation. "This is indeed a veritable treasure trove!"

"Ah – treasure implies monetary worth," Larkin cautioned. "Many of these items have little or no monetary worth. Their only value is in their history."

"And what better value could there be?" Mary went to a small table where pottery sherds were displayed. "I see that some of these have been accorded rough dates," she said.

"I have some small knowledge," Larkin admitted, taking up one small piece. "This one shows markings that date it firmly as of Viking origin. See the scratched outline of the longship? It puts it somewhere between 350 and 600 AD. It may have arrived here from the old Danelaw for all I know."

Mary wandered to another shelf and pointed to the two bronze bowls. "I see that you have yet to attribute a history to these."

"And that is because we have yet to decipher the markings," Larkin said. "Both have identical lettering, but those letters mean nothing to either of us."

"May I examine them?" Mary reached out for one of the little bowls.

"Please – any help that you may give would be very welcome," Larkin stated.

Mary searched the little bowl, turned it upside down and saw for herself the markings. "Tib, Mise – and three other marks that are indecipherable," she muttered to herself. She put down the bowl and went very quiet.

"Some idea is rattling about inside my head," she spoke quietly, almost to herself. "Have you somewhere quiet that I may sit and think more?"

"We can do better than that, can we not, Jamie," Larkin smiled at her. "Please, follow me to the hall where a comfortable settle, a warm fire, and a glass of mead may assist your thinking."

It was close to dinner when Mary came back into the large museum room.

"From the look on your face, your thinking has yielded results," Larkin observed. "Please tell us these results."

"It may take some time in the telling," Mary warned. "And to be utterly truthful, they are as yet mere conjecture – I cannot offer definitive proof."

"Then, please join us for dinner and we shall be delighted to hear what conclusions you have reached," Larkin led the way to a small dining room where a dinner was being laid out.

Mary laid down her knife after sampling a rather delicious dish of lamb. "I must take you back to the early days of the Roman Empire," she began. "The first real emperor was Augustus Caesar. His grandson was called Tiberius – and Tiberius was emperor at the time of Jesus' later life and crucifixion."

"And you attribute the letters TIB to Tiberius?"

"In isolation, I would not dare to put this forward as an explanation. But what follows – MISE – adds considerably to the hypothesis. He was born in an area near Naples that the Romans called Misenium – what we today refer to as Miseno. The more I think about it, the more convinced I am that these bowls are from the time of his reign. How they came to be on Dartmoor, I have not the slightest idea. Obviously, they come from a time when that empire stretched throughout the land they named Britannia – and that did not happen until many years after Tiberius' death. His son, Julius, sent many legions north to Germania, Francia, and Britannia. It may well be that one of these senior men brought with him the bowls that harked back to Tiberius' reign."

"And when did that reign end?" Jamie asked.

"As far as my memory serves me, 44 AD," Mary answered.

Larkin carried on eating for a while, then looked up again.

"We shall label these bowls as being from the reign of Tiberius, born in Misenium, as postulated by Mary Cove in the year 1667." he announced. "You shall have full recognition of your invaluable thinking."

Mary blushed slightly, extremely pleased to have contributed to the fund of knowledge that would be enshrined in the museum.

James and Avril had been making plans for some weeks before they announce them to Rosie. James was not far short of his fifty-eighth birthday, Avril two years behind him. They had been operating the apothecary shop in Bovey Tracey for over thirty years, making small strides forward in knowledge and development of new treatments. They had weathered seven winters of the horrible fever that came to plague the town, had saved innumerable lives and had mourned those they had been unable to save.

Mary Cove (then Ramsey) had been their very first 'apprentice', learning and becoming highly proficient at healing, before marrying Harry Cove. Nell, the little orphan they had adopted had become Mary's successor, also becoming highly skilled at the art of diagnosis, before marrying Adam and going to live in Newton Abbot. And then had come Rosie. Gil's and Ella's daughter and niece to Mary. Rosie had proved equally as successful as her predecessors. James introduced the subject as he, Avril and Rosie sat down to a late supper.

"You may well have wondered how long we intended to continue this work," he said, looking directly at Rosie.

Rosie's face turned very serious. She *had* wondered, her great-aunt and great-uncle were getting to the age when many thought of an easier life. However, she had not dwelt on it as she did not like to imagine what the town would be like without them.

"Well, we have been making plans," he continued. "You, Rosie, are just about as well prepared as anyone to take on the task. But you will certainly not be able to cope with it all on your own. So, we have been casting a very quiet net around the town to see who might come and assist you. I am very happy to tell you that we have indeed found someone."

"But without you, there will be a very sad lack of expertise!" Rosie countered.

"Oh, believe me, we are not just going to disappear overnight," Avril took up the story. "No, we have a much longer-term plan in place. There is one young girl in this town who is very well placed to come and learn. Would you be surprised to learn that Rachael Smith is eager and willing to come?"

"Rachael? Indeed, I would be very surprised," Rosie answered. "She has never said anything of the kind to me!"

"No, she would not have," Avril grinned. "She would have been embarrassed to mention it. But willing and very eager she most definitely is!"

"What we propose is that the two of us stay for two more years as we and you train her in every aspect of the healing business. By the time those two years are up, she will be sixteen and, hopefully, as competent as she can be. And then, and only then, shall we retire and leave the entire business in your capable hands."

"But what if she falls head over heels for some young man and marries him? After all, Rachael is a very pretty girl!"

"And what if you do the same?" James countered.

"Oh, I shall never marry," Rosie said firmly.

"And is that not what Nell said?" Avril chortled. "But there she is, a married lady with one child and another on the way!"

"But I mean it!" Rosie stated. "My life shall be devoted to the health and wellbeing of the people of this town."

"As has mine been – and I am married!" Avril could not help pointing out. "Marriage is no barrier to pursuing a career as an apothecary. Meet the right man and he will encourage you to remain as you are. Mary found it no barrier. She married Harry and he encouraged her to become the schoolmistress – and look at what a success she has made of that!"

Rosie was still not convinced. The prospect of soon becoming the town's senior medical person was far too large for her to contemplate marriage!

The three surviving members of the Sane and Sensible met at the rectory that same evening. Larkin, Kent, and Forbes sat around the fire and sipped appreciatively at glasses of a new wine to them – a pink-coloured wine from Portugal that was being called by its French title – Rose.

"Seems a trifle insipid," Kent muttered. "But there is no doubting its underlying flavour!"

"You, young Matthew, are becoming a wine snob!" Forbes chuckled.

Larkin took another sip and smacked his lips in appreciation. "I like it," he announced. "I just wish I could say the same for the court. As far as I am concerned, this court and its looseness is a severe disappointment. Believe me, I am no stiff-necked prude; I appreciate a laugh and a joke as much as the next man. But the way that some of the members of the court behave fills me with something close to revulsion!"

"Its display of immorality is nothing short of a national disgrace," Kent snorted. "How many illegitimate children has our king fathered to date? Ten? Fifteen? And still not a sign of an heir to the throne!"

"He has made some of them dukes of this place and that, countesses of other places. Soon, every seat in the Lords will be occupied by his bastards!" Larkin agreed wholeheartedly with Kent.

Forbes, remembering his once close association with the king, when that man had been the young Prince of Wales, found it increasingly difficult to counter these charges.

"Can it be that he is badly let down by others, who lead him astray with their own behaviour?" he attempted.

"No, that does not wash!" Larkin said adamantly. "He is the king, not a mere disciple of an ill-mannered group of fops! He should not follow but should lead – that is if he has the strength of character to do so. However, I sincerely doubt that he has. If he had that strength, he would not be fathering children upon all and sundry!"

"If this continues, Charles shall be succeeded by his brother James, Duke of York. He is a totally different character. He is a good soldier and a great leader. Moreover, he is married to Ann, daughter of Clarendon, and has legitimate children – and none illegitimate, or none that anyone knows of," Kent added.

"Aye, he was always a very serious young boy when I knew him," Forbes nodded.

"Then I propose a motion for consideration by the Sane and Sensible," Larkin went on. "That this house is, to say the least, disillusioned by this king and his court!"

He raised his hand, followed immediately by Matthew Kent – then more slowly by James Forbes.

The following day saw yet another visit by Nell to Bovey. This time, a very smart pony and trap drew up outside the apothecary shop. A very large man dismounted and carefully lifted a heavily pregnant Nell to the ground.

"A flying visit only, this time," she gave Avril a hug. "Oh – let me introduce Joseph. Adam refuses to let me travel anywhere alone. Joseph works at the docks for Adam and escorts me very safely everywhere I go."

Joseph, a man in his middle thirties, gave Avril a grin and a nod of a large head. His face was deeply scarred from temple down to the right side of his mouth. He pointed a deprecating finger at the disfigurement."

"Legacy from Tangiers," he explained. "Looks horrible, but not as horrible as the devil who gave it me!"

"As long as you keep our Nell safe, we care not a jot who you are or what you look like. You are most welcome," Avril gave him a smile.

"Believe me, mistress, she is in the very safest of hands," Joseph busied himself with the pony as Avril ushered Nell into the shop where she was greeted warmly by James and Rosie.

"Well, business must be good if Adam is able to purchase that lovely pony and trap for your conveyance – and to release an obviously well-trusted man from his work to accompany you," James declared.

"Indeed – business could not be better," Nell answered, removing cloak and gloves. "Believe it or not, Adam is now engaging a fourth vessel as a demand for granite blocks has just been placed by the sheriff of York. What he needs them for, we have not been told."

Avril then told Nell of their plans for their slow retirement. Nell expressed the same surprise as had Rosie.

"Rachael?" she exclaimed. "I should never have thought her a likely trainee!"

"As neither Avril nor I would have," James agreed. "But there is absolutely no doubt that she is as keen, nay determined, as you, Mary, and Rosie were. We are in no doubt of her commitment."

"But, to a matter that stares us in the face," Avril laughed. "How goes it with the babe?"

"Everyone says that, as I am carrying him low, it shall definitely be a son."

Avril regarded her adopted daughter. "I am no midwife, but it has been said for hundreds of years that the lower the bump the more lusty the boy. How does Kate take to that piece of knowledge?"

"She is delighted whether it be boy or girl. If a girl, she looks forward to becoming a second mother. If a boy, she anticipates a devoted slave!"

"Then she may well be disappointed!" Rosie grinned. "I made it my business when very young to make Jamie into my personal servant. It did not work!"

After a hasty dinner, Nell said goodbye to the woman she had always regarded as her mother, and to the man she had looked to as her stepfather. Joseph brought the pony and trap and helped Nell onto the seat beside him. Nell directed him to drive up the street and to stop at the church.

On her knees by the side of her father's grave, Nell whispered an update of happenings – as she always did when visiting the cemetery.

"Dada – never ever fear for me. I am as happy as I could ever have dreamed. Adam is still the perfect husband, and your granddaughter Kate is well and flourishing. This little one inside me will join a contented and loving family. Bless you as always and rest in peace with the mama I never knew."

AUTHOR'S NOTE

I have made much of the sense of disillusion felt by my imaginary characters. They had lost a king who was, to our modern way of thinking, a prude and full of self-righteousness. They had then inherited a parliament that was just as straightlaced. And then had come the Restoration of monarchy in the shape of Charles II. It soon became clear that the strictures of his father and then of parliament were a thing of the past. In its place came self-indulgence, merrymaking, permissiveness – on a scale that had never been envisioned.

Charles, by the time of his death in 1685 – eighteen years after the close of this story – had fathered fourteen illegitimate children – and those were just the ones acknowledged. How many more there were, borne to women of 'lesser' status, is simply not known. To a population that was mostly ardent Protestant, this was very odd to say the least. Many thought him a merry rascal; others believed him to be an unprincipled lecher. Three and a half centuries later, it is not relevant for us to come to judgement – we did not live in their times or 'burdened' with their beliefs!

I have also brought into the story the very unpleasant matter of the slave trade. It started to grow some years before my story began. It is believed that the first to 'trade' in this manner were the Portuguese. Whether this is correct or not, many men of business in mainland Europe and Britain were soon engaged upon one of the most financially profitable enterprises ever thought of. Bristol and Liverpool – to name but two ports - flourished on the trade, as did many of their merchant venturers. Many state coffers bulged with the income generated.

I have also mentioned three characters from the Restoration government. Lord Clarendon, Lord Arlington, Lord Ashley-Cooper. A couple of years after my story ends, these three were joined in association by Lords Buckingham and Lauderdale. These five, Clarendon, Arlington, Buckingham, Ashley, and

Lauderdale, became known by a five-letter word taken from their initial letters – CABAL. This is a very ancient word of Hebrew origin and refers to any secret group that engaged upon its own secret purposes.

Many people believe that the five were the originators of the word. They were not. They just, by their initial letters, became the inheritors of something regarded as secret and (perhaps) not to be trusted. Later, this grouping and their successors became the embryonic Tory party.

Please accept my sincere thanks for going along with my Bovey saga. The next instalment jumps another eighteen years. A Time of Revolt concentrates upon the happenings at the start of the short reign of James II.

Jim Marshall.
Devon. February 2024

Other titles by this author

THE BOVEY TRACEY SAGA SERIES
A Shameful War
A Time of Confusion
A Time of Acceptance
A Time of Change

Jamie's War